C.S. Boag is a former journalist who has also grown potatoes, driven taxis and bulldozers and worked in a hamburger bar. He has travelled many times throughout Australia and to France, speaking enough French not to die there. He was a Sydney City Councillor for six years and holds degrees from NSW and Sydney universities as well as postgraduate qualifications from Macquarie. Besides publishing short stories he has also worked as a columnist for *Woman's Day* and the *Bulletin*. He won the Walter Stone Memorial Prize for Literature in 1986. C.S. Boag lives on a small 'green' holding near Bathurst, NSW, with his wife, Judith. He has five children. www.csboag.com

Praise for Mister Rainbow

'Mister Rainbow is that rare creature – a PI with depth. Down at heel, shabby, inept – he's a born loser, at his best when the odds are stacked against him. Somehow, in a taut contest, he wins.' Barry Oakley, novelist and former literary editor of *The Australian*

'A must for lovers of the detective thriller. The hero's name is as thought-provoking as is the style of writing itself: quirky and challenging, with an underlying sense of humour which is both dark and memorable. Each of the first three books in the series was hard to put down and leaves the reader anxious for the next.' Belinda Kendall-White

'Living the life of a man off the grid – an occupational hazard – this private eye knows how to stay undetected. Since he is a master in the art of detection and has been in the game for no small amount of time, he has become quite adept at existing only when necessary, the rest of the time being spent in a myriad of dress, station, and persona.' Courtney Whittamore

By the same author

The Case of the Hood With No Hands

The Case of the Death of a Ladies' Man

The Case of the Horses for Corpses

The Case of the Bullets at the Ballet

C.S. Boag

MISTER RAINBOW

in the Case of the COCK ROBIN KILLER

XOUM PUBLISHING

Sydney

First published by Xoum in 2014

Xoum Publishing
PO Box Q324, QVB Post Office,
NSW 1230, Australia
www.xoum.com.au

ISBN 978-1-922057-88-4 (print)
ISBN 978-1-922057-89-1 (digital)

Cataloguing-in-publication data is available from the
National Library of Australia

Word count 57,000

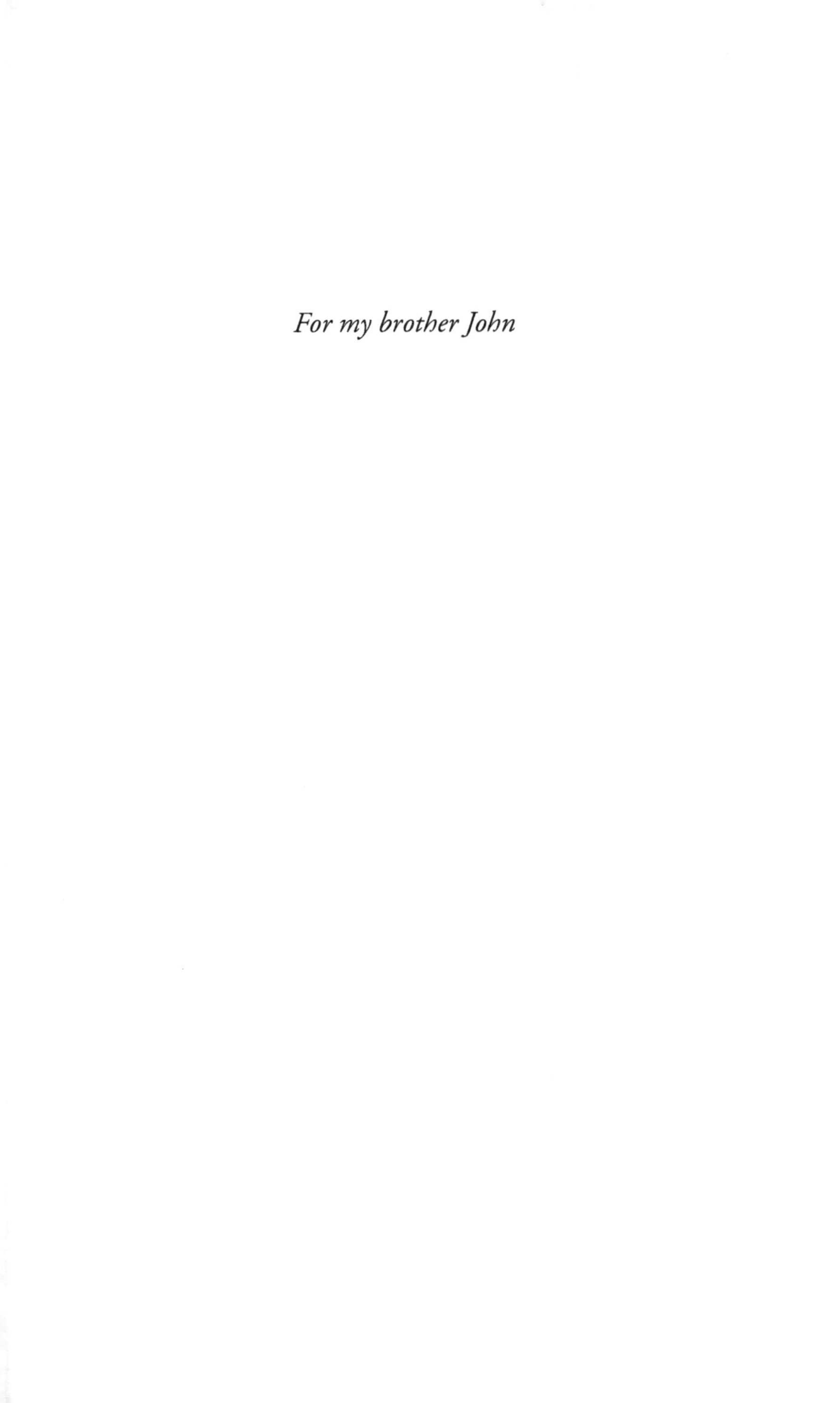

For my brother John

Chapter 1

BLOOD ON THE LABORATORY FLOOR

Queen's boat bumps alongside the old tub I call home – the *Wooden No*, as in, *What's she called? Wooden No* – disturbing the early morning calm along with my equipoise. He's called Queen because his real name is Freddie and the outboard powering his clapped-out boat's a Mercury. 'Here's your *petit dejeuner*, sweetie!' he sings. Something flops at my feet. *'Buon appetito!'*

He's off before I can thank him which is fine because I don't intend to. I finish my exercise routine, do the ballet warm-ups, prime the pump that keeps the *Wooden No* afloat, rinse my armpits with bilge water, clean the flounder and weigh myself on the scales – the ones from Vinnies, not the piscatorial kind. Then I strap on the shoulder holster while the fish sizzles on the Port-A-Stove, preparatory to keeping my appointment.

A dame in her distracted fifties directs me to the basement of the townhouse in Alexandria. The joint's a mess and the broad behind the professor is blonde, beautiful and in a state of disarray almost as bad as the laboratory. She adjusts her lab coat as she bends over a cage containing a two-metre diamond python while the professor – a grey-haired joker with blood on his collar – produces a big smile and an even bigger handshake. I accept the smile but not the handshake.

'I'm Professor Ransom and I called you in because the police – or at least the representative provided – seemed much more interested in my assistant than the break-in.'

The prof's assistant is what's known in the trade as a buxom wench – the body in the coat's like air trying to escape from a balloon – and she straightens as much as a dame like her is ever going to straighten, smoothing the coat while her lips form the shape of a Petrie dish.

'I'm Grace Metalious,' she says, holding out a hand like a wish-fulfilling prophecy. I accept both the hand *and* the wish.

'As Professor Ransom's assistant,' she goes on, 'I attend to all his needs – experimentally speaking. I see you've noticed the door off its hinges ...'

Yeah, I noticed the door off its hinges. I also noticed a lot else besides: the overturned work bench, the smashed rodents' cages, the overfed snake, the scattered remains of the lab mice, and the blood. Especially the blood.

'Must have been quite a party,' I say.

Ransom shakes his head. 'It was no party. My lab adjoins the marital home and on Thursday night I heard what sounded like a break-in so I hurried down to investigate.'

'The marital home being that of you and Miss Petrie Dish here?'

Ransom does a nice impression of a laugh. 'Oh, no, no, no and no again! I'm a happily married man while Grace here's my laboratory assistant.' I find myself wondering if Grace here could ever be nothing but anything. 'Having said that, I must add that she's very good at what she does.'

'Which is?'

He's a grown man but he still colours.

'I'm a behavioural scientist researching high-rise home units: why people buy them, what people like in them – basically what sells. Like me, Ms Metalious is a Pavlovian – I'm sorry, I should explain: Ivan Pavlov was a scientist who worked out why dogs dribble –'

I've strung him along enough. 'How much time elapsed between the lab being broken into and you investigating?'

'Well, I'm fit for my age.' He glances at the dame, presumably for confirmation. 'So it couldn't have been more than a minute or two.'

'Where was your wife at the time?'

'Asleep, I presume.'

'Don't you know?'

'We sleep separately. That is, in separate beds, in separate rooms, on separate floors. There was no noise from Mavis so I presume she was asleep.'

I leave his words dangling like a body on a roadside gallows in a high wind before doing the follow-through.

'And when you arrived you found all this damage?'

He nods. 'It was absolute chaos.'

'Who has keys to the laboratory?'

The grey eyebrows rise; he's a scientist; he's worked it out; why can't a detective?

'Why ask about keys?' He indicates the door. 'After all, the place was quite clearly broken into.' He shrugs. 'I'm sorry, the answer to your question is: Grace and I.'

'What did she do?'

'Who – Mavis?'

'I'm sorry, did I say *she?* I meant *they* – the vandals.'

'Oh.' The scientist frowns. 'Well, they released our experimental rats and Betty – that's the *Morelia spilota spilota*, the diamond python we keep in order to dispose of used rodents – ate them. It's pointless vandalism.'

'What – feeding rats to a snake?'

'No,' the Professor replies. 'What the vandals did. We had almost completed our research when it happened. Our records were stolen, which means we'll have to start again from scratch.'

That must be the scratch that resulted in the blood on his collar.

'Which, of course, will take time,' I say. 'Who do you think did it?'

'You tell me. After all, that's why I called you in.'

'Hazard a guess.'

He shrugs. 'Kids maybe; or someone who hated either me or the developer who employs me.'

'Who knew about your research?'

'Just Grace, Mavis, me and the developer.'

'Who's the developer?'

'Ivan von Franck.'

All I know about von Franck is what I read in

the papers. But if what I read is only half right, it narrows the suspect list to just about everyone else in Sydney.

Chapter 2

NINE TIMES OUT OF TEN IT'S THE WIFE

I switch tack or tack switches, however you want to play it.

'Tell me about the marital home.'

The boffin waves a white-clad arm past the broken-down door. 'It's where I live with my wife.' I nod; the wife would be the dame who directed me to the lab while wringing her hands like she was doing her husband's dirty washing. 'We've had thirty good years together and – thanks to this work and the fame and fortune it will bring – we can look forward to a good thirty more.'

'That's nice.' I glance from the assistant to the snake to the blood. 'But it must be tough on the rats.'

He frowns while the assistant goes on straightening the empty cages.

'It's for the greater good.'

'What – flogging expensive apartments to punters that can't afford them?'

'I'm a scientist, with a scientist's values. What people do with my findings isn't my concern – my interest lies solely in the research. Now if you can't help me –'

'Oh, I can help you all right. It's just a matter of

whether you're going to fully appreciate my help or
not.'

'What do you mean by that?'

'I mean I've worked out what happened. But
before telling you my findings, I'd appreciate
payment up front.'

The scientist has brought cash like I instructed
him to and, while he's extracting it from his
laboratory coat, I spot something on the floor of the
snake cage, step across, open the door, pick up what
I saw, pat the overfed serpent on the head, and close
the door again.

'I'm something of a student of human behaviour
myself,' I say, 'only I don't need birds to arrive at my
findings.'

'But we don't use birds.'

'What's this then?'

I hold up the red feather I found in the cage and
the scientist puts on a set of half-moon specs before
whipping them off again because they make him
look older than he probably wants to in front of his
assistant.

'Why, that's a feather from the *sternum* of a male
of the species *Erithacus rubecula* – otherwise known
as a robin redbreast.' He frowns. 'It's a native of
Europe although there are some in Sydney, having
been introduced by the early settlers. Where did you
find it?'

'In the cage with the anaconda.'

'But this is a scientifically controlled environment.'
His frown clears. 'But, of course – the bird flew in
after the door was knocked down, only to be eaten
along with the rats. What are you implying?'

'Something different from what I was about to suggest – but only marginally. You see, at first I thought – as I was no doubt meant to think – that the break-in was committed by someone who didn't have a key.' The professor and his assistant exchange glances. 'Which would rule out both you and Grace here because you both have keys. Which means I was supposed to think that the break-in was done by someone else, someone who released the rats and the snake, leading to the wrecking of the lab, and afterwards departed with your findings – all before you got down here a minute or so after you heard the break-in. Which would have been extremely smart of the intruders.'

The scientist looks uncertain. 'Yes, it would, wouldn't it.'

'Not only smart but also impossible,' I continue. 'You see, Professor, you were too quick off the mark. Unless, of course, the destruction occurred *before* the door was broken down, having been carried out by someone who had a key.'

'Wh – what do you mean?'

'I mean I believe I was supposed to think that your wife – after learning of your affair with Grace here – broke into the laboratory and –'

'What affair!' the professor shouts. 'This is preposterous! Really, I'm not paying you to –'

'– discover the truth? But I thought that's just what you *were* paying me for – you being a scientist.' I indicate Grace. 'She's beautiful and that stuff on your coat isn't blood, is it?'

Absent-mindedly, the professor rubs at his collar.

'It's not what you think. I don't employ Ms

Metalious for her beauty. She's a highly intelligent woman with a string of letters after her name as long as –'

'... as long as the snake I'm supposed to believe your wife let loose after breaking down the door and destroying your work and taking your records in a fit of pique over your affair?'

'It would be the end of our marriage if she did,' the professor says.

'Yeah, it would, wouldn't it? Under normal circumstances – given this little triangle is in any way normal – you wouldn't have left your wife in a fit. Because like most husbands in your situation, you think you can have your cake and eat it – keep both nooky and cookie. But Grace here didn't agree, so – hoping to prolong her employment as well as the relationship – she took matters into her own hands, let herself in with her key, wrecked the joint, and *afterwards* broke down the door to make it appear that ...' I leave it there; the prof's a bright boy; he can work it out. 'Grace is certainly big and strong enough to bust down a door, whereas your wife ...'

He's ashen-faced. I like them ashen-faced – it means I might have put out the fire.

'Grace here was relying on that old chestnut: *Nine times out of ten it's the wife.*' I hand the boffin back the dough-ray-me. 'Under the circumstances I can understand if you want to let the matter drop and under the same circumstances you can have your money back.'

I don't have to open the door because there's no door left to open. So I just tuck the feather in the holster next to the gat, straighten my *chapeau*, give the anaconda a parting nod and make myself scarce.

Chapter 3

I WANT SOME RED ROSES ...

I put his height at close to the two-metre mark and he's in our way like he belongs there – a mountain of muscle in a dirty singlet, pink shorts and mismatched thongs. When you're that big you don't have to worry about fashion. Once, Aunt Rube would have taken him with her eyes shut. But once, too, this was public land covered with gum trees instead of skyscrapers and you could see where you were going without using a periscope.

After I arrive at Rube's – the aunt-cum-detective who took me in and taught me how to be a private eye – she unhitches herself from her kidney machine and we go for a walk through the Botanical Gardens.

'They want to develop all this,' she says. 'Which means there'll be even more ghastly hotels and visitors' centres and no doubt yet another casino.' We cross College Street and enter Hyde Park, bearing westwards. 'They call it progress,' she continues after a while. 'The Hotel Australia once stood there with its glorious staircase and stained-glass windows, and men with manners in the vestibule instead of the thugs you see today. Buildings had awnings to protect you from the elements and gentlemen doffed their hats when they met you. Just there was the Hotel Metropole, catering for the sons of graziers in town for the Show.'

'So what happened, Rube?'

'Greed and corruption happened, Rainbow. I'm not saying things were better, they were just — different. It was easier being a detective back then because there was a well-defined line between good and evil. But that line started to go fuzzy until now there's no line at all. It's the same with development — people seem to build anything they want wherever they want.' Aunt Rube's sigh advances all the way up from her corn-cob toes.

I shrug. 'Where's this taking us, Rube?'

'The walk or the talk?'

'The talk.'

'Well, I've taken on a case, see, and ...'

Rube used to be the scourge of every bent cop in Sydney, plus anyone else unlucky enough to cross her path. She was the best at tracking down errant husbands, exposing blackmailers, locating stray kids — solving anything from petty theft to murder. But detecting is a hard game and Rube's no longer young. And since the kidney problem resulting from getting thumped in the *Bullets at the Ballet* caper, she's had to keep herself pretty well caseless.

'I thought you'd hung up your gat.'

'It was just a little job for Madam Blavatsky.'

When Dad dumped me after Mum topped herself — taking my sister with her — Aunt Rube taught me the basics of detection: induction, deduction, abduction, gunmanship and dance. Yeah, that's right, *ballet* – to get me out of those tough places private eyes can find themselves in – and my dance teacher was Sydney's *belladonna* of dance, a refugee from the eastern Caucasus, a mammoth dame who gave lessons on the top floor of a terrace in East Sydney, just around the corner from Aunt Rube's hovel.

'I didn't know Madam B was in the building game.'

'She's not,' Aunt Rube replies. 'Nor does she want to be. But someone's trying to force her to sell her place in order to complete a zillion-dollar development block, only Madam B won't budge. Which puts her in the shooting gallery. Let's say there have been threats.'

'What kind of threats?'

'The usual. It'll escalate into pillage, arson and murder, but at the moment it's still in the gentle preliminary stages – people following her, threatening phone calls, anonymous messages, the odd visitor.'

'So Madam B asked you to –'

'Madam Blavatsky didn't ask me to do anything. I just happened to be playing piano for one of her dance classes when a rock came hurtling through the window. The window was closed at the time.'

'Why were you playing piano?'

'Because Madam Blavatsky asked me to. Which reminds me – I can't play tonight. Could you fill in for me?'

A song's stuck in my head: *I want some red roses for a blue lady/Need them for the sweetest girl in town.* The words don't fit the situation but it doesn't stop the music. In the armpit-sized nursery called *The Greenhouse Defect* the stench of crocuses mingles with the scent of the recycled animal remains they use for fertiliser.

'Hi, Bone,' I say to the dame lurking behind the aspidistra.

Bonnie – that's her real name, the distaff side of Bonnie and Benito, sometimes known as Bonnie and Clyde but to me just plain Blood and Bone – smiles.

'Hi, Rainbow. I take it you want some roses. You got woman trouble again?'

I like Bone. She's got a cross-painted mouth and her dress sense is right up the spout, but she calls a watering can a watering can and doesn't take nonsense from nobody, and that includes me – only cash.

'You could say that.'

'I just did.'

The Greenhouse Defect is an oasis in the desert, a verdant refuge among too many coffee houses atop Darlinghurt Hill. They used to hang ten-year-olds in Darlinghurt just for pinching handkerchiefs. Now spaced-out art students lug bedraggled canvases, prostitutes try to look alluring, and mad buggers with knives roam the streets looking for an excuse to rob people. I blame the coffee.

'I'm after a couple of dozen long-stemmed reds, thanks, Bone – with the thorns off.'

'It's that bad, eh?'

I discovered Bone when things started going wrong with Salina, the mother of my fifteen- – or is it seventeen-? – year-old daughter Imogene. In other words, right from the opening salvo of our relationship. I bought a lot of flowers and as a result got closer to Bone than an assassin to the heart of darkness.

'It's worse,' I reply as she gets to work with the paring knife. 'You see, I took this dame to France and –'

'That'd do it.'

'It was *work*, Bone.'

'That'd do it even more.'

There's a conspiracy among women and – nice as she is – Bone's part of it. Dames latch onto an inconsequential fact and, like a dog attached to a postman, there's no shaking them. All I did was take a beautiful dame called Hell and Damnation – sorry, that should read *Hélène Dalmation* – to France to help rescue my daughter.

'You missed a couple of thorns, Bone.'

'Why don't you just forget them?' she says, wrapping the roses in cellophane the colour of blood. 'You know, after too long in this game I've come to the conclusion that some men are cut out for relationships and some aren't. And you're one of the ones that aren't.' She hands me the flowers with a soiled hand and an extra big question mark. 'Forty bucks for you, Rainbow.'

'How much for anyone else?'

'Twenty-five.'

'Put it on the tab, would you?' She starts to take back the flowers; I flick her a fifty. 'Just kidding. You can keep the change.'

Chapter 4

... FOR A BLUE LADY

Darlinghurt used to be my playground. Rube lives there and I attended the primary school there, until she hauled me out because of the bullying. It doesn't pay to be a kid with a name like Rainbow in a place like this. Madam Blavatsky's dance studio is in East Sinny, a suburb that lies buttock-by-*gluteus maximus* with Darlinghurt, but it's half an hour until I play piano. My friend Annie does volunteer work in the Men's Refuge in Sanctuary Lane and it's dinnertime. I need to pay her a visit.

You're asking for trouble carrying flowers in Darlinghurt. Hannah is astride the wall outside the old Christian Science Church on Liverpool Street and chucks me a smile overcut with cocaine, swinging a bare tootsie at the end of a leg that doesn't seem to have any top to it.

'Who's the lucky girl, Rainbow?' she purrs.

I shrug. 'The way I see it, having me in the frame makes her unlucky.'

'I wouldn't mind putting my shoes under your bed.'

'You haven't got any shoes.'

'Doesn't stop me not minding.'

The Refuge reeks of booze, sweat and long-dead marsupials, a cross between a ferret house and a collective of camels. A couple of hundred deadbeats slouch at plastic-coated trestle tables while volunteers dish out the food. One of the volunteers is Annie, the pretty little number who once upon a time was my squeeze.

'You got a moment, Annie?' I ask, the flowers behind my back.

She's wearing a pink apron over khaki coveralls and the expression she puts on is somewhere between *Who are you?* and *Go to buggery.* She pushes past me bearing a tray of sausages and I follow, gripping the flowers. A dero lunges for the food, but Annie holds the tray over her head and frowns even more than she was already.

'Are you drunk, Tony?'

'Me?' The derelict grins around the room before returning his mud-stained eyes to Annie. ''Course not.'

'Because if you are I'm not serving you – you know that, don't you?'

It's like she's talking to a baby – a baby with devil-clawed fingers, cadaverous cheeks and random rows of stumps for teeth.

'Yeah, *Anno Domini,*' he answers meekly. 'I know that.'

'Then you'll also know to take your hand off my tray.'

The drifters are squid adrift in a sea of helplessness, the dregs of the heady concoction that goes to make up Sydney society, the muck that everyone pretends isn't at the bottom of the barrel.

'I'm sorry, Annie.'

'It's better not to do bad things than have to say you're sorry.'

She hasn't changed her tone from when she was speaking to the dero, or even her words.

'But what did I do?'

'Everything you've ever done is what you do, Rainbow. You come into my life, disappear out of it, then turn up again expecting everything to be normal. Well, you're right, everything *is* normal. Because normal's when you're more interested in your cases than in the people close to you, and I've had enough.'

I wave the flowers around Hell's waiting room; life-wrecked faces stare back like fledgling birds wondering where their next worm's coming from.

'But this is what *you* do and I've never complained about it.'

'Why do you think I do this, Rainbow? Have you ever thought about that?'

'What's there to think?'

It's the wrong answer in the wrong place at the wrong time. Annie turns her back again and this time it's a rock wall. The last I see of the rock wall is it crashing through a pair of *faux*-bar doors into a steam-filled kitchen full of ghostly and barely discernible figures, among whom Annie also becomes ghostly and barely discernible herself.

The steam makes the flowers wilt and my eyes mud.

As darkness creeps over the mean streets the world changes and it's not for the better. Druggies stare out of ice-crazed eyes, night girls scream and drunks urinate in doorways, while the over-rich cruise by in their black sedans taking what's in it for them. Next to a green-baize door in a terrace islanded in a lot of vacant land surrounded by chainwire looms a large sign reading *BLUEBEARD DEVELOPMENTS*.

Bluebeard was a serial wife killer which makes the name especially disturbing. There's a disturbance on the stairs, too, as I let myself into Madam Blavatsky's. I toss the flowers, go down on one knee and drag out the gat – the blow-back, single-action Beretta – the only kind of squeeze I've got these days. A 40-watt bulb lights up a lump on the stairs. I can't hear any feet shuffling on the floorboards above, there's just the figure under the blanket with nothing to show for itself but a pair of Nikes. I nudge the lump with a whiteside.

'I'll pay …' it mumbles.

Yeah, you'll pay all right, I tell myself, if you haven't already. But I don't say anything out loud as I gather what's left of the flowers, step over the figure and hurtle up the stairs, the gat switched to *SHOOT NOW AND ASK QUESTIONS LATER*. The ground floor's derelict; the second's where Madam Blavatsky lives; and the top floor's the studio where she teaches dance. I hear her voice, shelve the gat, push open the door with the mitt that's not holding the flowers, and go in.

The wide, bare dance floor's still ringed by two wooden barres with an old, cracked washbasin in one corner. There's the old wraparound mirror and a bunch of leotard-clad kids that once included me sitting cross-legged on the floorboards. The baby grand's a Steinway and Madame Blavatsky's perched on a *chaise longue.*

'I escaped from a terrorist regime,' she's saying, 'so I know that life's no more than a temporary respite from death. I want you to carry that thought with you when you dance.'

Madam B's the heavy metal of ballet. When these kids go to bed tonight, all bar the most insensitive are going to have nightmares. The parents won't be happy but Madam B doesn't care what people think.

'This is Mr Brown, girls and boys. He's an ex-student and tonight he's going to be playing piano.' She frowns. 'And while it's nice of you to bring flowers, Mr Brown, they look much like most of these kids dance – terrible.' She sighs and takes the roses across to the basin. 'But I'll put what's left of them in a vase.'

What's the difference, the Steinway asks, *between a buffalo and a bison?* Answer: *You don't wash your hands in a buffalo* … I like Steinways – they speak to you. And what this one's saying – apart from the bad joke – is: *People might be temporary but some are more temporary than others.* It's a thought that accompanies the riffle-raffle of kids getting ready to dance to the music of Strauss.

'All right, children,' says Madam Blavatsky, placing the vase with the roses in it on the piano, 'it's dance time. Raeleen, take off those silly earrings – this isn't a fashion show. Harold, extend your fingers. Position, position, position!'

I crack my knuckles over the keys as Madam B

raises her arms. It's hard to tell if she's about to belt the kids over the head or conduct them.

Just then the door bursts open. Immediately, I go into a crouch and haul out the gat. But it's just the figure who was curled up on the stairs – I can tell by the shoes – checking to see what all the fuss is about. And after he takes it all in, he shakes his head and wanders off again. But not before I see the look on Madam B's face – the kind of look a kid might get when the Gestapo come for her father.

Chapter 5

THE PIANO PLAYER

I go back to playing the piano and the kids finish their *arabesques*, *battements* and *pliés*. Some are good and some are terrible and nothing will ever change that, no matter what Madam B does. After the kids pack up and leave, Madam B collapses onto the *chaise longue* like a stabbed tyre, like everything's suddenly got too much for her.

'Are you going to tell me what this is all about, Madam B?' I mean, you're talking death to the kids; then there was your overreaction to the figure at the door –'

'You mean *our* overreaction.'

'I'm talking about *your* problem, Madam B, not mine.'

She shrugs. 'And it's just that, Rainbow – *my* problem.'

'I might be able to help.'

'I don't need your help.'

It's the attitude of someone who's made her own way in the new world after making her way out of an old one that consisted largely of blood, hate, organised suspicion and sanctified crime. I indicate the empty piano.

'Where is she?'

'Who?'

'Your piano player.'

'She broke her arm.'

'She wouldn't have done that playing Chopin.'

But I'm not getting anything out of Madam B so I take a gander at her address book under the pretext of helping with the clean-up. Under *Piano Player* I find a name – Gertrude Match. It comes complete with the honorific *Miss* and an address that's almost as bad as the name. I realise Madam B's behind me – she moves quiet for a big dame.

'What are you up to?'

'Just helping with the clean-up, Madam B.' I flick the address book shut and get myself to the door where the remaining rose petals look like blood. 'Be seeing you.'

She chucks me one of her looks, the one with a lot of suspicion in it.

'Not if I see you first, Rainbow.'

The figure's no longer on the stairs but as I move along the street I'm conscious of a shadow. All right, East Sinny's all shadows but this one's got substance to it – probably a prohibited one. I turn my back – one day I'll deal with Pandora but not yet – and on the turn I see the sign.

Your eyes play tricks on you around here. People think they see daemons with clawed fingers and monsters with humps on their backs and wild-eyed devils wielding pitchforks when all it is is other people just like you. I got it wrong. The name of the developer's not *BLUEBEARD* but *BLUEBIRD*.

It puts a whole new construction on things.

Piano players aren't the sharpest notes on the keyboard so it doesn't surprise me to find Gertrude Match occupying a hovel in Miller's Point – that's *Miller's* with an apostrophe, whatever the name changers say – a suburb that once harboured the Black Plague but has graduated to being a refuge for indigents and indi-ladies.

The figure behind me ducks behind a wall as I open the rickety gate leading onto a verandah, find what looks like a malignant skin mole with the word *PRESS* on it and do like it says. After a few seconds, the door opens revealing a dame with multi-coloured eyes, a shapeless frock made of sky-blue calico, and a plaster cast stuck out in front of her like a forklift.

'Miss Match?'

She peers at me through the fly-wire. 'Who's asking?'

I want to say *Mister Perfect* – in which case we're a perfect match – but instead I palm her a card through a hole in the fly-wire. The card tells anyone who wants to know that I'm a private investigator called Harvey Flite, contactable at *harveyflite. etcetera.com.au* or by leaving a note at Harry's Bar, allowing seven days for a reply – unless it's an emergency, in which case it'll take longer. And at the end:

'The name's Rainbow.' I give my real name
because Miss Match knows Madam B and at
some point they're going to compare notes; but
the dame's already reading the card so I explain
the discrepancy. 'Okay, so the name's different and
the contact details are someone else's but the word
INVESTIGATOR means what it says and I'm here
on behalf of Madam Blavatsky.'

The face on the other side of the fly-wire looks
only marginally gayer.

'Why would Madam B need a detective and what
would a detective want with me? All I do is play the
piano.'

I indicate the forklift. 'Correction: *used* to play the
piano.'

When the dame shrugs, her prong rears up like it's
operated by hydraulics.

'I was hit by a bus.'

'Yeah, and I just got hit by a suspicion.'

'Which is … ?'

'That if you were hit by a bus, Mismatch, you'd be
covered with bruises and contusions, and you'd have
at least one broken leg and a couple of broken ribs
to go with the leg. Yet there's no sign of any damage
other than your arm. Which means you've not only
got a selective injury – you're also selective with the
truth as well.'

'Wow – you must be a detective.'

'And you must be lying. Are you going to let me
in, or do I make like Santa and come down the
chimney?'

It gets me the shadow of a smile. It's a start.

'Why should I let you in?'

'Because I can help.'

'I don't need help.'

'That's not how it looks from the outside.'

'But there's not enough room in here to swing a cat.'

'That's okay, because I'm not here to swing cats.'

Chapter 6

A DISTURBANCE IN
THE STREET

Due to the presence of a spinet, a stand containing a music book and a marker pen, and half a cubic inch of air between us, it's standing room only in Mismatch's house, so we stand. But after a while she loosens up enough to park herself on the piano stool while I make my own arrangements – sitting on a chair that would benefit by being chopped up for firewood.

'Sorry if I interrupted your rendition of Rachmaninoff's Second,' I say.

'You recognised the tune!'

I indicate the stand. 'No, I read the name on the music.'

'Oh.' She looks disappointed; she also looks like she's changed her mind. 'I'm afraid I don't have anything to drink ...'

I drag out my flask. 'That's all right: I travel armed. All we need is drinking bowls.'

She goes into the kitchen and returns with a couple of jam jars. 'Very well, I'm ready for the interrogation, Mr Whoever-you-are. What do you want to know?'

'How you broke your arm,' I say, pouring her a double.

'I fell.' She glances at me, then down at her jar, before changing her story. 'All right, it happened in East Sydney; people get their arms broken in East Sydney.'

'No one's ever broken mine.'

'That's because you're male and you're lucky.'

'Like I said, Mismatch, yours is a selective injury. So what I'm guessing is that someone broke your arm and at the same time issued you with a warning: *Don't go to the cops or anyone like the cops* – meaning people like me. Which is why you look nervous and also why you're not telling me the truth. *Make sure Madam Blavatsky knows about it,* they would have added. *But the merest whisper to anyone else and it's your Last Waltz.*' I apply the heat. 'Someone followed me.'

The dame's face turns whiter than her plaster cast. 'Who?'

'If I knew that, I wouldn't be here.' I lean forward – that way she can see the gat. 'The jokers that broke your arm were standover merchants – push-men for someone with a lot of pull in this city. There's a sign outside Madam Blavatsky's that says *DEVELOPMENT* and it's not hard to see that her joint's in the middle of a development site. By itself, Madam B's place is worth no more than a slug in a week-old corpse – but as part of a building site it's worth a mint.'

'But why break *my* arm over it? It's not *my* property.'

'You came out of Madam B's. They might have thought you were her.'

'Come on, Mr Flite, she's twice my size.'

I shrug. 'Like the Bard said, *The medium is the message.* And your arm was the medium.'

'So it was a warning to Madam B …' Mismatch's multi-coloured eyes contemplate my ordinary ones over the mug that tells me she's out of her depth. 'What do you want to know?'

'I want you to tell me who did it.'

'The little one.'

'Could you be more specific?'

'Only if you give me another smile-maker.'

I do like she says and after another swill or two she fills me in on the blind side of her ten-fingered concerto. She was playing piano for Madam Blavatsky when she was interrupted by a disturbance in the street.

'Come on, Mismatch, we're talking East Sinny. There's always a disturbance in the street. It would be disturbing if there *wasn't* a disturbance.'

The dame holds out her mug for another refill. 'Except that it wasn't prostitutes screaming or addicts howling at the moon.'

I top her up.

'What was it then?'

'The sound of music.'

'What kind of music?'

'A *doof-doof* kind of music, played *fortemente* – that means loudly.'

'So you went to investigate this loud music …'

'I'm sorry, Mr Flite, but unlike you I'm not an investigator. The children were up to that bit in the ballet *Les Sylphides* where they dance off to church to the strains of Chopin. It's nice, gentle stuff, but because of the noise it was impossible to continue so

Madam B called it a night and I left.'

'Just you?'

'We finished early and the children had to wait for their parents, so, yes, I left alone.'

'Even though we're talking East Sinny?'

The dame laughs. 'Oh, Mr Whatever-your-name-is, you're such an innocent! I was married to a brute which is why I live in a hovel. Compared to my ex, the streets of East Sydney are child's play. You can always escape from a mugging but … Anyway, I left on my own, even though it was East Sydney.'

'Where did they get you?'

'In the arm.'

'I mean where were you – streetwise?'

Chapter 7

RHAPSODY IN BLUE

The dame suddenly sobers – but that could be the wrong word. 'Sorry, it was a foggy night so I couldn't see my hands in front of me. If I had, it would have been the last time for a while, I suppose – I mean, think … Anyway I was almost at the noise when I realised it was a recording. I thought it was a student prank. It was quite an elaborate setup, with witches' hats, plastic tape stretched between them and speakers the size of wire doors.'

'All this just to mug you?' I ask.

'I didn't – still don't – know what they were up to. But didn't you say they were after Madam Blavatsky?'

'Make that *might have been*. Describe them for me.'

As she talks I'm only half-listening because I'm imagining a surreal situation with the dame bright-eyed and innocent in the middle of something she couldn't possibly understand. And I'm also wondering how – with her arm like that – she manages to cook, eat, sew, clean house, undress herself and take a shower. Such thoughts are part and parcel of how a detective's mind works but right now they interfere with my hearing.

'What did you say?'

'As I said, there were two of them, a tall, skinny one and a short, fat one and they stepped out from behind the speakers and … It was dark and there was no-one else around. It was like the the locals knew what was happening. The small one wanted to know where St Vincent's Hospital was. When I asked why, he said someone's arm was broken and when I asked whose, he said mine …'

'How did you react?'

'I learnt not to scream when I was married.'

'How did they do it?'

'The big one stood behind me and held my arm out and the little one had a cricket bat …'

'Did you see their faces?'

She stands, raises the seat, scrabbles out the drink that she said she didn't have, lowers the seat, passes the bottle to me and shakes her head. I knock the top off the bottle.

'In East Sydney, there are no street lamps because people use them for target practice. As well as that, as I said, it was a foggy night and …' She takes a mouthful of the new malt. 'Also they were wearing masks.'

'What was their height?'

'Breaker Morant was small while the other one was tall.'

'Describe their voices.'

'The little one didn't speak.'

'And the other one?'

'His voice was unnaturally high. But in the end, all I got were the masks, a broken arm and a name.'

'What was the name?'

'Lofty.'

The one behind was tall; it figures; I still ask. 'Which one was Lofty?'

'The little one.'

After the attack, Mismatch returned to Madam Blavatsky's, who got her to hospital and after that … But after that there's only one thing I need to know.

'How come you were playing piano when I arrived – considering you're wearing finger boards, a fact that would preclude your playing?'

She smiles her crooked smile and her bi-coloured peepers go crossed. 'I was wondering when you'd get to that, Mr Flite.' She spins the stool using her *extensor breva digitora* and *glutea maxima* and reels off a few bars using only her feet. 'This spinet doubles as a pianola – it contains a roll of paper which is turned by the foot pedals which acts on a mechanism that activates the hammers. All I have to do is pump the pedals.'

After a while we exchange seats – a difficult manoeuvre given the limited space but somehow we manage – and, using my hands and not my feet, I play George Gershwin's *Rhapsody in Blue*, that nice quick-slow, soul-sinking number with the emotional kick in the middle. Before I go, I pick up the pen from the music stand and – in letters much like

those on the sign outside Madam Blavatsky's – I
write: *Somewhere there's a bluebird of happiness* and
sign it: *Rainbow.*

Chapter 8

OUT IN THE COLD

The cicadas are humming as I climb off the omnibus but clouds are gathering. After I cover the remaining two kilometres to 21 Castanet Close the cicadas have shut up and the first drops of rain are falling. The door's as tight as a miser's wallet, and the footsteps coming down the hall possess all the enthusiasm of a eunuch at an orgy. The door opens and my ex-wife Salina – also known as Aetna because she can erupt without warning – is staring stilettos at me. I make the request before the eruption.

'Could I see Imogene, Sal?'

'She's not here.'

'I just thought me and her might –'

'No, no, no and no again!' She grips the door and her eyes are bullets. 'If you expect me to be grateful because you saved Imogene, you've got another come thinking.' The word placement tells me she's upset, if I didn't know already. 'I only went to France because I was desperate to escape from you. Which means it was your fault Imogene was ever in danger.'

It's not the way I saw it – Salina went off to France with her lover and took Imogene with her. But like the good book says: *There's a time to be born and a time to die; a time to get and a time to lose; a time for logic – but this isn't one of them.* Sal warned me away from Imogene; this is my first visit to Castanet Close since the *Bullets at the Ballet* caper.

'We would just have a little *patisserie* …'

Salina's knuckles whiten while her attitude darkens. 'I don't want Imogene anywhere near that tart of yours.'

'If you're referring to Annie, she's no longer on the scene, she …'

'So what are you going to do — go to the police and tell them you're Imogene's father and want to see your kid? They'd just say: *We hear a voice but we can't see anyone. It must be the stress of the job, all these ghosts.*' Sal shakes her head and my confidence along with it. 'You haven't got a leg to stand on, Rainbow — or arms, body or even a head because, by your own wish and volition, you're a non-person. *I've got no birth certificate, no licence of any kind,* she mimics, *therefore I don't exist …*'

She pauses for breath. Even Salina's got to breathe sometimes.

'But if I call the cops, suddenly you will exist,' she continues. 'You'll have a face and they'll put a name to it and you'll be thrown into jail for not existing. You mightn't be aware of it, Rainbow, but people aren't allowed not to exist. You're breaking the law by not existing and can only get away with it by remaining a non-person. Because once you come in from the cold — which you'd have to if you want to see Imogene — they'll get you. Which means, of course, that you can't.'

'But, Sal … !'

'I'll tell you one time, Rainbow, and one time only: you might be the father but being a father is pretty much an irrelevancy these days, more so in your case. You're as substantial as the phenomenon your dopey mother named you after – nothing but coloured air. But you still need to hide from the cops as well as everyone else. You think not existing is a kind of freedom and maybe it is. But that freedom's got a price, just like everything else.' My ex-wife pauses – as much for breath as for effect. 'And that price is your daughter.'

I check the hallway behind her but all I can come up with is memories.

'You can't see her because as far as you're concerned she's not here – metaphorically, literally and in every other way. You don't exist, so how can your daughter? And if you *try* to exist – if you try your trickery-dickory surveillance routines or a kidnap – you'll end up seeing nothing but the inside of a jail.'

There's one last thing. There's always a last thing.

'But you still have to pay for her upkeep. Whatever society might say, she's still your child, and children don't come cheap.'

I start to say I never intended not to pay but Salina's already closing the door. On the about-turn I'm greeted by the ice-cold reality of rain.

These days, you can't do much without a phone, besides which I want to see Rory. But by the time I arrive, the rain's hammering on his newly-renovated hovel – a façade of speckle-brick cardboard over common-and-garden fibro, an imitation-tile roof and a front garden fresh out of *Reader's Dingbat's Confused Homes* – complete with fake crazy paving and gaily-painted gnomes. Rory doesn't take off the security chain when he opens the door so I keep my side of the dialogue bright and breezy.

'Hi, Roarer – long time no see!' He stares like I'm a disease; I force a grin. 'I need a phone, Roarer. Hey, it's cold out here – are you offering an old mate shelter from the elephants?'

Rory frowns at the rain.

'What elephants?'

'As in: *Nor rain, wind, thunder, fire, are my daughters: I tax not you, you elephants.* Although it's really *elements* … it's from *King Lear*.'

Rory's puzzled, but Rory's always puzzled. 'From *what*?'

'Shakespeare's *King Lear*.'

'I thought a Lear was a jet.'

'He was also a king.'

'No,' he says.

'What do you mean, *No*?'

'I'm not offering shelter to an old mate.'

'Why not?'

'Because we're not old mates.'

'Come on, Roarer – we could hardly be described as *young* mates! Which means –'

The head above the hand behind the door nods.

'You got it – it means we're no longer mates.'

I know the reason but I still ask.

'Mind saying why?'

Behind Rory I can hear Janet – behind every ex-hitman is his missus. Rory met Janet in *The*

Hood with no Hands caper and it went downhill from there: he got hitched and found God – not necessarily in that order – and Janet sees me as the Devil incarnate which means that Roarer does, too. Which also means that the door doesn't open any further than it has to, while Rory launches into a diatribe.

'You use the word *mate* like it's some kind of *Open Says-To-Me* but that only works if we're mates. But we're no longer mates so the key no longer fits because I've changed the locks. I donated a kidney to your Aunt Rube which gives me a direct projectile to Heaven but I'm not resting on my barrels. There's going to be no more killing. And we're no longer mates.'

I shrug like it doesn't matter. 'I still need a phone.'

The voice behind Rory bounces off the new furniture that goes with the new house in much the same way as the rain goes with my mood. 'Dinner's ready, Sweetie-Pie!'

'I'm coming, Sugarplum,' Roarer sings back and when his eyes return to mine they're deader than his erstwhile victims. 'Try the morgue. Tell 'em Rory sent you, ask for Goldilocks and say you want the usual.'

Chapter 9

ANOTHER STIFF RECEPTION

It could double as a public inconvenience – a grey blockhouse crammed between a Toyota showroom and a developers' club in the inner-city suburb of Glebe – and the sign above the door says anything but *MORGUE*. A blonde eyes me out of a goldfish bowl, in a room with a washable floor.

'You Goldilocks?' I ask her.

'No,' she replies, with even more suspicion than she had when I arrived. 'You a delivery?'

I shrug. 'I was told to ask for Goldilocks.'

If you weren't dead when you arrived here you wouldn't have long to wait. The air alone could kill you. This is Death's tradesman's entrance – unpainted bricks, a cracked ceiling and the barely breathable stench of uncut formaldehyde. There's too many doors, the arse-end of an air-conditioner and a room labelled *RELATIVES WAITING* – forget the apostrophe. A black-haired joker with too many pens in his shirt pocket emerges from behind one of the doors.

'Who are you?' he asks.

'I'm whoever I am – what about you?'

'I'm Goldilocks.'

There's no point asking about the hair and how it fits in with the name; I'm an in-and-out kind of guy and this is an in-and-out kind of place.

'Rory said to see you about a phone.'

The waiting room's an alcove, a short hall and a room with a stiff in it. The stiff's seen better days – one eye's missing, her throat's been slashed and her lipstick's crooked. She's got nothing to say for herself and even less when Goldilocks reappears carrying a sack over his shoulder, which he dumps on the corpse's feet.

'Don't mind the stiff,' he says. 'It hasn't got anything to do with anything. Corpses come and go.'

'Rory said …' I begin.

'Good old Rory,' Goldilocks replies. 'Did he say how we met? I was standing in York Street contemplating suicide when a bus mounted the footpath. I thought – make that *hoped* – I was a goner. You see, according to my religion, suicides don't go to heaven. But if I happened to be taken out by a bus I was hopeful I'd be categorised a non-suicide … In that brief moment a lot of thoughts went through my head – none of which involved survival. But that was before Rory saved me with his crutch.'

'The brand of phone doesn't matter,' I tell him.

'I wasn't grateful.' He settles the sack and makes himself comfortable; like the stiff, Goldilocks looks to be settling in for the long haul. 'You see, suicide – and I'm a suicide counsellor, so I know – requires a great deal of courage. But courage is a quality I don't possess. The bus took out a blind man and a dog, yet I survived. I wasn't happy and when I was finally able to speak that's what I told Rory. Do you know what he replied?'

'I'll pay cash.'

'He said: *Think of the paperwork you saved*.'

'Any age, any brand, any condition,' I carry on, oblivious to his story. 'As long as it's got a few kilometres left on the clock.'

'It was like Rory knew what I did for a living. If you could call this a living.' He pauses. 'Anyway, when Rory said that, I just about cacked myself. It was a long time since I'd had a good laugh. I'd been scammed of my life savings, my wife had left me and my pet cat had carked it, so me and laughter were strangers. Then this bloke says: *Think of the paperwork*. Later, after I'd got to know him, I realised what Rory was saying — which was that, while life's serious, you've got to have a bit of fun while you're living it. But that was before I discovered what *Rory* did for a living!' Goldilocks shakes his head.

'One's plenty,' I tell him.

He looks like he's just noticed me. 'Of course, you want a phone.' He rummages in his sack. 'These are all legit, by the way — cops give them to me and I find them on corpses like Madam Slash here.' He palms me a fistful of *Telefunkens*. 'Ah, a watch with a compass in it — you might as well have that, too.' He rummages some more. 'And here's the *piéce de resistance*.' He's brandishing a near-new Samsong I-Spy. 'It's one of those clever phones that does everything but dance the tango and whistle Dixie.'

It's pink and there's a patch on it that might once have been blood.

'This is a death from unnatural causes,' I say. 'Mind telling me how it happened?'

'The subscriber stopped breathing.' Goldilocks shrugs. 'Does it matter?'

'It might.'

Goldilocks checks the tag on the phone. 'I remember: it was a murder that the police weren't interested in, which is how we ended up with the phone – the case, you might say, was *dead and buried*.' He checks to see if I get the joke; I do but I'm not encouraging him. 'There was a suspect but she was never charged.'

I sense that the phone's trouble. I could say *No* to it, but for some reason I don't. 'Any other details?'

'It belonged to someone called' – he rechecks the tag – 'Cock Robin Fahey. From memory there was something *odd* about it all.' Goldilocks fiddles in the pocket with the pens in it. 'Here, take this in case you want the file.' He hands me a card that says *SUICIDE COUNSELLOR* along with the mobile. 'I switched off the phone to save the battery and also the contract's still got legs on it.'

There are contracts and there are contracts. The phone's cold. So is the joker's hand.

'How much do I owe you?'

Goldilocks shrugs. 'Like I say, everything's got its price, but for a mate of Rory's –'

I cut across him. 'We're no longer mates.'

'All right, for an *ex*-mate of Rory's everything's got its price. But what I'm giving you happens to be free.

I should add that the story I told you is a load of baloney – due to the nature of my work I tend to romanticise. I really met Rory when he delivered one of these.' He gets off the cot he's been sharing with the stiff, hefting the sack after him. 'I'm a trained shrink, by the way, so feel free if you're ever in need of counselling.' He winks. 'Just joking.'

I pocket the phone and decant myself from the morgue before I die laughing.

Chapter 10

THE PHANTOM CALLER

The strand of cotton is still stretched between the hatch and the top of the jamb, and the right-hand corner of my well-thumbed copy of *Crime and Punishment* is exactly where I left it – on the *Wooden No*'s map table in conjunction with the first point of Aries.

I swill out the bilge; clean, fuel and restart the pump – remembering to top up the oil; check the hull for fresh leaks; and wipe the bird dung off the bow. Then I haul out my new pink Telefunken and switch it on.

Immediately there's a machine-gun *rat-a-tat-tat* that's got me hitting the deck before I realise it's some smart-arse jim-crack's idea of a ringtone. I hit *Speak* – and get silence. The little window says it's a silent number. It figures.

'Yeah?' I say.

More silence. I got a connection but that's all. Then beyond the throb of the pump and the yelp of seagulls, I hear a noise that sounds like sniffling – which in turn is drowned out by what sounds like the beginning of the end of the world.

'Who's there?' I ask, abandoning my phone rule of not speaking unless spoken to.

But there's still no answer – just the tail-end of

the noise that sounds like the end of the world and, closer to home, the sniffling.

I got two choices – ditch the phone or keep it – and I feel some connection to the phone so I keep it. No-one knows I'm the new owner – no-one, that is, except Goldilocks at the Morgue. But I've still got the feeling I'm covered with fleas – the kind of itch I get when I'm being followed, the feeling that someone's out there that shouldn't be out there, when in all likelihood …

Stalkers are a constant companion in this game: disgruntled husbands, thwarted lovers, killers crossed in the course of an investigation, the cops, other private defectives – as well as, in my case, my nemesis, Pandora. So I do what I always do: make a security sweep – checking the superstructure for hidden cameras, the cabin for listening devices and the rest of the boat for sensors of any kind. And after I find nothing, I take a bottle of Glenfiddich onto the *Wooden No*'s roof, pour myself a double and ask myself if it's worth it – to which the whisky replies in the affirmative.

That's when the *rat-a-tat-tat* begins all over again.

At first I think it's the chopper that happens to be passing overhead. But the rattling continues long after the whirly-bird's gone and I realise it must be the phone. Left to its own devices, the mobile lapses into silence. I watch a launch chug towards the open sea, the sunset turn Sydney Harbour into a bloodbath and pour myself another whisky – only to drop the bottle when the phone rings again. The phone belonged to a corpse. Who'd call a corpse? I click on.

'Who's … this?' a querulous, female voice asks. Dames of a certain age say *Who's that?* not *Who's this?* which suggests she's young. There's a nasal quality to the delivery, so she's got a sinus problem. Apart from which, there's no rising inflection, which means she's sure of herself – except for the hesitation.

'I'm someone answering a phone,' I reply. 'Who are you?'

'I asked you first.'

Most of the time when the wrong person picks up – and as far as this dame's concerned I'm the wrong person – they say, *Sorry, wrong number*, and click off. Instead, the voice on the other end of the line wants to know who I am.

'Like I told you the first time,' I say carefully, 'I'm someone answering a phone. Who are you?'

'I can hear sea noises,' the phantom voice replies, 'water lapping against a hull, seagulls …'

I get that feeling again. But as well as checking the boat, I also checked the phone and there's nothing in it that shouldn't be. Then I remember what Salina said, and after that, what Goldilocks said: everything's got a price. And I find myself wondering if the caller might be a dead subscriber who's suddenly realised she's got time left on her phone, ringing to ask for her money back …

'I don't need to know who you are,' I lie.

'Nor do I have to say who I am, because I'm not the person with the phone.'

'What difference does that make?'

The voice doesn't say. Instead it asks, 'How come you've got it?'

Everything's got a price. And in this case that price

could turn out to be death, except the phantom caller doesn't sound like a killer. But like Aunt Rube and experience have taught me, killers come in all shapes, sizes and voices. Killers don't have to sound like killers.

'How come you're asking now?'

'Because the phone's been turned off but now it's turned on again.'

Which means the caller has been trying this number regularly, often, *frequently*, which gives me the answer to the question of *who* she might be – if not *why* she's calling. Which means I know pretty much what I want to know and, by leaving the phone on, I'm only giving her the chance to get what *she* wants – whatever that might be. So I switch off, pour myself a triple, and try to enjoy what's left of the blood on the water.

Next morning, with the Harbour as flat as I feel after a night on the hops, I stare at the cabin wall and try to put a face to the voice on the phone the previous night. It was low-slung, soft as silk but with an edge to it – like the silence a knife makes after it hits the wall next to your head. The boat swings 180 degrees and a shadow crosses the cabin. I climb out of the bunk, get up the companionway, blink into the harsh light of a new day and make myself a coffee on the Port-a-Stove. And after I bail out the boat, fill the pump with fuel and oil and restart it, and the position of the sun over South Head tells me *normal* people are heading to work, I grab another phone and dial the number that Goldilocks gave me.

'Death-watch beetle here.'

Like the man said, you got to laugh.

'You said you could get me the court records that go with the pink phone.'

'Pick up or delivery?'

I tell Goldilocks delivery.

'What's your interest in all this?' Harry asks.

I shuffle the newspaper out of the way so he can park the bucket of sludge he calls coffee where it can do the most harm. Then I tell him about Rory, Goldilocks, the phone and the phantom caller. He puts on his *you-got-to-be-kidding* face.

'Except it's not about the phone, is it, Rain? This isn't about a *damson* in distress or some anonymous caller or the desperate need of a modern-day *Don Quixote* crusader-detective to right wrongs, because right now you haven't got a wrong to right.'

He pours himself a cup of coffee out of his personal squeezebox.

'You're interested in this whole caper because you need the distraction, right?' He rubs the table with a rag even dirtier than the table. 'Your aunt's crook, maybe dying; Rory's told you to go to buggery; Little Orphan Annie's given you the brush-off; and your ex-wife's acting up even worse than usual. You're conflicted and that's the real reason you want those records.'

'Ever thought of turning detective, Harry? With those eyes of yours and that razor-sharp mind you could be another Perry Mason – all they'd have to do is cut off your legs.'

'I'm just saying you ought to stick to cases that come your way, not go shopping for them. You don't know what you're letting yourself in for.'

I'm happy to take my chances. Just like I'm prepared to take a risk with Harry's coffee, even though there are some things you shouldn't do if you want to stay alive.

Chapter 11

THE LAST WITNESS

A headline distracts me but I feel like being distracted. It takes up most of the front page:

SYDNEY IN THE DOLDRUMS
Developers to the rescue
Exclusive by JOHN CURTIS
'First they complained about Barangaroo — that magnificent development soaring proudly from the old Sydney docks on the western edge of the city. The same wimps and fairies that want to live in the Dark Ages got up in arms about plans to develop the Botanic Gardens and the Domain. After which there was all that fuss about developing the disused dog track at Wrigglesworth Park. And now ...'

I continue reading because it's a distraction.

'... Sydney would still be a backwater containing nothing but gum trees and kangaroos if not for our far-sighted developers. Men like Ivan von Franck are the modern-day explorers — the Burkes and Wills and Leichhardts and Edward John Eyres of the 21st century — men who risk their very lives ...'

There's more in the same vein — the sort of vein that,

if it was in your wrist, you'd slit it. A codger goes to sit at a table but Harry waves him away, sags into the chair next to mine and hunches over his *cross-ant* and coffee. I tap the blatt.

'What's this about von Franck risking his life?'

'Ivan von Franck has crossed more people than your average priest has crossed either himself or the line into moral turpitude. As for him risking his life – well, this is the building industry where most of the time the only thing on the level is the floors, and even then ...' He wipes a crumb from his mouth. 'Some unionist got up von Franck's nose and died and people reckon von Franck was responsible.' He flaps a hand at the blatt. 'That journalist,' he adds, indicating Curtis' byline, 'is an honourable exception.' He pats the pocket of his apron. 'I nearly forgot – someone left this for you.'

The court papers are court papers and the people in them say what they typically say. It's not the truth but a coroner's court is a court of law and a court of law isn't interested in the truth so much as in people's ability to avoid it. I try to put myself in the minds of witnesses but it's like a play with no surprises because the dialogue goes according to the script. And at the end, the coroner rules:

I believe that the police in this case – particularly Detective Sergeant Richard Richardson – did their best to determine the identity of the murderer. But so far they have been unsuccessful. I am therefore bound to find that the deceased met his end at the hands of a person or persons unknown …

I go over the cast of characters and always and forever come back to the same name. For a start, it belongs to one of the few dames in the case. And for a finish, she appears to be one of the few jokers in the pack who actually want to solve the murder.

Please tell the court your full name and address.
My name is Carmen Maria Blenkinsop and I live …

I half-expect her to be told the correct word is *reside* but if there's an interruption it's not recorded. Instead, she's asked:

What was your relationship to the deceased?
I was his wife.
Would that be in the traditional sense or de facto?
I'm sorry?
Were you or were you not actually married to the deceased?
As I said, I was his wife.
Magistrate (intervening): *You're being asked if the arrangement was a common-law union or one espoused by the Church.*
Does it matter?
Yes, because this is a court of law and we are concerned with the truth.
Then I suppose we weren't actually married …
We have to steer clear of suppositions – were you or weren't you?

*We weren't but aren't we trying to find out who
killed —*

That's enough, witness. Next question, please.

There's more of the same — too much more of the
same — but none of it gives me that nice, warm
feeling I get when I'm learning something worth
knowing. Why, for instance, did the dead man die?
Who killed him? And who was my phantom caller?
I've got a name but no idea if she's short or tall, fat or
skinny, likes cats or possesses a squint. She's as much
a mystery as the identity of the person who killed
the husband who wasn't a husband, and the only
surprise is the witness who makes his appearance
near the end of the proceedings.

Please state your full name and address.
My name is Ivan von Franck …

Chapter 12

MAKING A KILLING

If a name crops up twice in one day it's not because the elements have conspired or the planets are aligned or the cat ate the canary – in my book, there's got to be a reason. Also, there's an address for the dame – courtesy of the court papers – so I catch a blue Government bus with grey-speckled windows so that outsiders can't ID the passengers. The bus driver's radio is tuned into someone called Shockman Jock.

JOCK: We've got Trevor from Verdant Vale on the line. Thanks for joining us, Clever Trevor, it's great to have you with us. We're interested in your views on people who – ha, ha – make a killing in the building industry.

TREVOR: Yeah, well, people should be allowed to make money, shouldn't they? I mean this is a free country with free entry-prizes and everything ...

JOCK: That was meant to be a joke, Trevor – I was talking about all the murders.

TREVOR: All what murders?

JOCK: Thank you, Trevor. (Hangs up.) Bloody idiot. Now we have Mavis from Matraville. What do you think, Mavis?

MAVIS: I agree, yeah, Trevor's a bloody idiot.

JOCK: I mean what do you think about all the killings?

MAVIS: Hasn't there only been one?

JOCK: I'm speaking journalistically, Mavis. We might have heard of only one but where there's smoke there's sure to be some arson around – that's a joke, Mavis. What I'm saying is: Should there be an inquiry into the building industry?

MAVIS: No, let the bastards kill each other. Just the other day, Tony was at it hammer and thongs with another dog and –

JOCK: I don't see what …

MAVIS: – and there was no way I was going to interfere, know what I mean? It's the same with these bathplugs. Let them rip each other's throats out. They're a bunch of thugs, if you ask me, and –

JOCK: Thanks, Mavis, but I didn't ask you. We now cross to someone with an opinion that is worth listening to – Mr John Curtis, of Sydney's Daily Terrorgraph. *How are you, John … ?*

I get off the bus in the middle of Peter from Parramatta saying they should bring back the lash and hoof it to the address given by the dead man's widow, a hovel next to a billboard featuring a cop with a camera promising: *MORE COPS, MORE CAMERAS, MORE CHANCE OF GETTING CAUGHT.* I knock on a door that's about as welcoming as the billboard.

'Is that you, Arnold?' comes a voice from within.

'No, I'm someone doing a survey. I –'

'And I'm the Duke of Edinburgh. Look, if you want money, I haven't got any. And if it's furniture you're after, there isn't any of that left, either. So bugger off and leave me alone.'

I wait.

'Look,' comes the voice again, 'I know you're still there because I can see you through the peep-hole. But I'm not opening up so you can bugger off.'

The stone step's rough and there's an even greater roughness to the voice behind the door; a roughness that says she's had enough; a roughness that implies that, under normal circumstances, she might be a nice person, but otherwise she's got a gun; it's also the wrong voice, so I do like it says and bugger off.

On the way back to the boat – a walk, another bus trip, a ferry ride, and finally a cross-country trek to where I beached the coracle – I switch on the pink phone and ring Aunt Rube. And Rube says that, while it's nice I phoned her, she happened to be enjoying a kip for the first time in weeks and I woke her. No, she's not interested in how I'm going with her case, just in sleeping. After which I'm even less reassured than I was before and my mind's a long way from where it should be as I return the phone to my pocket, flip the row boat right-side up, drag it into the water, find the oars and start rowing.

Night does strange things to boats and I've had too much to drink which makes it worse. Somewhere between waking and sleeping I find myself detached from my personal moorings, like I'm floating in space. And because my feet aren't on *terra firma*, I could be upside down or sideways or drowning. Distant noises seem close and the water lapping against the hull could mean I'm on a lake on the moon. I feel my consciousness drift with the boat. Fate laughs as something nudges against the bow. It could be a shark or a mackerel or a lost dolphin but the next bump's none of the above …

I hurl myself out of the bunk, drag on my pants and grab a gat – it turns out to be the Hoopla and Cock-a-Doodle .38 – and get up the companionway. As I make my way through the main cabin, I make out a shadow on the wraparound deck. There's too much cloud to see any detail but the way it moves tells me it's a dame. And in the absence of evidence to the contrary, I figure it's Pandora, my nemesis, who's been after me for as long as I can remember.

As I ease myself towards the hatchway, I've got the gun out but I'm also faced with the usual conundrum: what to do when we find ourselves face-to-face. I can't kill her because I don't know who she is and she hasn't hurt me – yet. But if she runs true to form she'll be carrying a knife. I don't know how she found me, and neither do I know what she'll do in a shoot-out. All I know is there's a figure on the deck and from its size and weight and the way it moves, it's no seagull …

I crouch beside the map table as I work my way through the possibilities. If it's not Pandora, it could be a drunk, a thief or a vandal. Like drowned crews, lost souls come and go on boats moored in Sydney Harbour, and with a bit of luck this one will go. Unless she's something to do with one of my cases – past or existing – someone I've crossed in a long history of crossings, or –

The figure's on the lee side of the boat – I can see its head against the night sky. The *Wooden No*'s an old flat-bottomed ferry which means that when she's not sinking she's stable and the tub doesn't move when the figure does, just continues to sway at its mooring, impelled by the movement of the sea. Weight of interloper, 130 pounds – 65 kilos in the new measure; height: five foot six, maybe seven; and she's slow but not scared – just careful. She reaches the back hatch. I make my move.

You die every day in this game. The trick is to watch your back and try to stay out of trouble. But that means applying logic to an illogical business. I'm sleep-stupid but that doesn't excuse the mistake. I'm on home territory but I forgot the bottle, the empty I dropped last night on the way to my bunk, the one I tread on now, my foot twisting to one side and my arms coming up like I'm surrendering.

A light as sharp as a stiletto cuts across my eyes and a banshee starts screaming. Suddenly, the figure's leaping down the companionway towards me. An instep gets me where I don't want to be got and I go down. The figure's above me and to my right and the light's full in my eyes. But she's an amateur. I lunge, my fingers find what feels like a calf, and I bring the interloper's leg up and sideways. The torch clatters to the deck and goes out, the figure goes down and I'm on top of her. She's soft and there's the strong smell of –

I don't do lights on the *Wooden No.* Show a light and it's an invitation to crash the party. So as my mind goes, I do what I do by feel. Hair – long and wet and done up hard against the skull; head neat and smallish – confirm it's a woman's; arms strong for a dame; waist a woman's waist, hips *ditto*; and the kind of thighs you don't muck around with unless the owner consents. This isn't a fight I want to be in and for a moment I ease off and a wave of nausea sweeps over me as I recognise too late the sweet-sour smell of the chloroform and feel myself go under.

Chapter 13

THE CONTROL FREAK

I come to trussed like a marrow, the early-morning sun cross-eyed against the *Wooden No*'s salt-encrusted eastern windows. I'd think it was a nightmare – except for the ropes and the dame seated on the wraparound bench opposite me.

She's not looking my way but gazing out at the bushland fringing the Harbour. Most of the tension is in her hands, one of which is clutching my gat while the other's holding the pink phone she filched from my pocket. She must have sensed me looking because she turns and for the first time I notice the nose. With her kohl-ringed blue eyes, golden hair and skin that looks like it would melt at a touch, hers would be a face of radiant beauty – except for the nose: at some point it's been broken and not reset properly. It should make her look bad but it doesn't – it just accentuates her beauty.

'We've decided to wake up, have we?' she says.

It's the voice on the phone, the one accompanied by the end-of-the-world sounds and the sniffling, the one that belongs to the dame in the coroner's court. Past the dregs of the chloroform I try to recall the name. Caramel – no. Carmel – no again. Carmen. Yeah, that's it, Carmen. *Carmen Ready-Or-Not* – Carmen Maria von Blenkinsop. No, not *von*. Just plain Blenkinsop. An unlikely name and an even unlikelier dame to have it.

'Carmen Maria Blenkinsop isn't your real name, is it?'

'No, I'm Minnie, and – for reasons that wouldn't be immediately obvious – they call me *Skinny* Minnie. Carmen Maria Blenkinsop was the name I gave the court.'

'Which leads me to ask the following question,' I go on. 'Why give the court a false name? It was only a coroner's court, nothing but a preliminary inquiry into a death, not a murder trial. Why lie about your name?'

'I was acting on advice.'

'You mean someone told you to commit *perjury*?'

She shrugs. 'As you said, it was only a coroner's court.'

'Who advised you?'

'Just someone.'

'Why didn't you answer the door?'

'What door?'

'The door to your house.'

'Why should I answer the door to my house?'

'Because I knocked on it.'

Skinny Minnie looks fazed and then quizzical – then we both pause. It's called a freeway standoff, when people find themselves on a median strip in the middle of an expressway with traffic speeding past in both directions and no way of getting to the other side without dying. The end-of-the-world racket on the phone was a plane taking off while the sniffling was … Yet neither of those factors pertain to the address given.

'No-one knocked at my door.' She looks confused. 'People never knock at my door ...'

'So as well as giving the wrong name, you also gave the wrong address?'

The dame nods. Something's not computing for her either.

'Again acting on advice.' She frowns. 'But the question I need answering is: why did you kill my husband?'

'What makes you think I killed your husband?'

She holds up the pink phone. 'Because you had this.'

It's the mobile from the morgue, the you-beaut pink phone with all the fancy trimmings, the one that Goldilocks assured me didn't have a price on it. Only now I'm discovering that it does.

'How does having your phone make me a murderer?'

'How else would you get it, except off his body?'

'I can explain ...'

'Can you?'

I struggle against the bonds but it's no good – the dame knows the ropes.

'How about untying me?'

'And let you kill me the way you killed my husband? That wouldn't be too bright, would it?'

'Except I didn't kill your husband.'

It's daylight and the Harbour's waking – a boat robber rows past looking for a boat to rob and a ferry thumps by in the direction of Manly. The early-morning oar-splashers have come and gone, but the dame's still with me.

She looks determined, I'm trussed like a rooster,

and she's got my gat. And if I don't give her what she wants, she'll most probably strap an anchor to me and chuck me over the side, and no-one will be any the wiser. That's the downside to not existing – you can't kill a non-person because he's already dead.

'You work for von Franck, don't you?' she asks me.

'No, I don't.'

'But if you don't work for von Franck, who do you work for?'

'I'm a private investigator.'

'A private investigator who does contract killings on the side …'

'No, I'm a private investigator full-stop. I right wrongs. And deaths on the side are wrong so I don't do deaths on the side. People might die but I'm not the killer. What I do is solve cases.'

'Like finding out people's names and where they live. Only you didn't do that very well, did you?'

'That was because my starting point was a lie.'

'As they say in the computer world: GIGO – Garbage In, Garbage Out,' Skinny Minnie murmurs. 'But while your old-fashioned methods didn't work, I tracked *you* down using modern technology.'

'So it was the phone …'

The dame nods. 'My husband was a control freak. He bought the phone and installed an app on his computer so he'd always know where I was.' She shrugs. 'It's just a blinking light. And as soon as you turned the phone on *and left it on*, I had you. All I had to do was go where the LED light led me.'

I've already worked that out. What I haven't worked out is why the dame's leaning sideways while

I'm sliding across the splintery deck towards the bow. A wind's sprung up and something's banging against the side of the *Wooden No* but that's no reason for the tub to –

Chapter 14

NOT ONLY
SLEEPING DOGS LIE

Skinny Minnie's making like a gimbal – one of those gadgets you use when you don't want your drink to spill – staying upright while the bench tilts under her. At the same time I feel myself slide and when I look out the window the trees are leaning and the horizon's at an angle it shouldn't be.

'We're going under!' I yell. 'There's a hole in this boat bigger than Fate and the pump's stopped. You've got to untie me so I can restart the pump.'

The dame shakes her head but the gun stays still. 'If I let you go you've got me. You're bigger and as a private detective you're undoubtedly far more unscrupulous. I'm not untying you, which means you've got to tell me how to stop us sinking or we'll both drown.'

So I tell her what to do and she puts down the phone and the gat, gets herself out on deck, lowers herself over the side, and restuffs the hole like I told her to. After which, I hear her refuel and restart the pump and I feel the old ferry begin to right herself as the dame returns, even wetter than she was before.

'You'll find something in the aft locker,' I say. 'You'd better change or you'll die of pneumonia.'

'What's it to you?'

'It's the normal concern of one human being for another. Also I'm trussed, remember.'

I look out the window and when I look at her again, Skinny Minnie's dressed neck-to-knee in oilskins, scraping her hair back and working out where to take it from here. She picks up the gun but I can see her heart's no longer in it.

'Where were we?' she asks of no-one in particular. 'That's right, I was accusing you of killing my husband and you countered with the accusation that I was following you. In the course of which it turns out you're a private detective who uses old-fashioned methods to find someone and fails.'

'I only went to the wrong address because you lied.'

She shrugs. 'Detection should be above lies.' She pauses. 'But as it turns out, you're right – I shouldn't have lied. If I hadn't lied, I could have got on with my life, secure in the knowledge that my husband could no longer attack … me.'

'What difference did lying make?'

'It made me vulnerable all over again.'

'Yeah, vulnerable to the person who told you to lie, the joker who's trying to seduce you – at a wild guess, I'd say it's the cop in charge of the investigation into your husband's murder.'

She turns wary. 'How did you know?'

'Old-fashioned detection methods. Only one person knew you were lying and that was the person who told you to lie. And he not only told you to give a false name and address – a lie that could get you into serious trouble, by the way – but also to dream up an alibi, *because he believed you were the murderer.*

His motive being to save you or put you in his power or both. Your adviser wouldn't have been your lawyer because – going by the court records – you didn't have one. That leaves the investigating officer – from memory, one Detective Sergeant Richard Richardson.'

For the first time, Skinny Minnie looks at me with interest. 'You're more than just a pretty face, aren't you? Which is just as well because you're not all that pretty.' It's an attempt at humour but I don't laugh. 'I suppose I should have got on with what was left of my life.'

'So why don't you, instead of hunting down people who happen to have your phone, in the belief that they *might* – just might – be your husband's murderer? The bloke might have been a dog but now he's a sleeping dog, so why not just let him lie?'

'You'd like that, wouldn't you? Seeing you're the murderer.'

The boat's on the level and it's about time we levelled, too.

'Look, Minnie, we could go round in circles like a boat at a swing mooring but you've got to get back to your baby.'

I've surprised her again and her eyes grow even darker than they were before.

'How did you know I had a baby?'

I shrug.

'There were three clues: the crying I heard on the phone; your hesitation when you said your husband could no longer attack *me* – you were going to say *us:* that is, you and your child and your increasing anxiety as feed-time approaches.'

A vertical line forms between Skinny Minnie's eyes like she's just thought of a possibility she hadn't considered before.

'You're not only a detective,' she muses, 'you're a good detective ...'

I can see where this is headed.

'No way,' I tell her.

'You're hardly in a position to argue,' she replies. 'Given this tub's going to sink, you'll drown if I leave. Which means you'll take on the case if you want to live. But before I employ you, how can I be sure you're not the killer?'

I take a deep breath and tell her the truth. 'Because I've got an alibi.'

Skinny Minnie grimaces. 'According to my late and unlamented husband, wrongdoers have alibis because they need them, while innocent people —'

'The transcript gives a date of death. Your husband was killed on —' I say the date. 'But it so happens I was overseas at the time, trying to save my daughter.'

That was in *The Bullets at the Ballet* caper; I was in France, something that's easy to prove — even using the outdated methods of an old-time defective.

'And before you suggest I might have employed someone else to do my dirty work, think about it. If von Franck contracted me to do the killing, I'm hardly going to use a sub-contractor, am I? It puts too many people in the loop, when the aim at such times is to keep things as close as you can.'

The dame waves the phone with the hand that's not holding the gun. 'So how come you had this?'

'It's a long story, Minnie. But cutting it short, my usual supply dried up so, acting on advice just like you did, I visited the morgue where I found no-one particularly interested in your late husband's belongings – including that whizz-bang *Telefunken*. So I scored the phone, a watch with a compass in it – and a widow.'

Chapter 15

GREY CLOUDS IN A BLUE SKY

Truth takes longer to sink in than the *Wooden No* takes to sink into the Harbour and the dame's stubborn, so I leave the sentence hanging along with my fate. I feel the boat lurch, which means the plug's already working itself free again.

'If I let you go, will you look for my husband's killer?'

'Have I got a choice?'

'You could promise, then break that promise after I untie you.'

'Which means you haven't got a choice, either, Minnie. Because:

You've found yourself a detective;

You need to feed your kid before it dies of hunger; and

If you let me go, the three of us have got a chance but if you leave me to die, at least one of us hasn't got any chance at all.'

She comes to a decision, parks the gat, unties me, steps back while I restart the circulation in my arms and legs, then picks up her pink phone but leaves the gat. After that, I row her to shore where she changes back into the jeans she left under a bush – along with the purse containing her fare home. She returns my wet-weather gear but hangs onto the phone.

'I'll be interested to see if you keep your side of the bargain, Mr Sailorman.'

I nod, concentrating on getting the oars in the rowlocks. 'You'd better give me your address – and this time make sure it's the right one.' I nod at the phone. 'Also you could leave that – I might need it.'

The explosion's one I'd prefer not to have witnessed –a *Whoomph!* followed by a lot of smoke and a sheet of flame. There's no time for fancy knots to secure the dinghy – nothing more than a hasty half-hitch over the stanchion – as I hurl myself onto the *Wooden No*, fighting my way to the heart of the conflagration: the pump. My first thought is the dame did it, while the second is I'd better put out the fire.

The heat sears my skin, lifts the paint off the hull and gets far too close to the fuel tank for my liking. By the time I get the extinguisher going, the fire's blazing. Other sailors keep away: it's the maritime code – if someone's in trouble, stay away until it's safe to help. By which time you should be even further away.

After the fire, the *Wooden No*'s even more of a wreck than it was before – black where it once was grey, charred where it used to only be rotten, and in imminent danger of ending up at the bottom of the Harbour. I check for signs of a bomb but there aren't any; look for a fire-starter but there isn't one of those either; then I examine the remains of the pump, to discover the dame didn't top up the engine oil when she refuelled – either because she didn't know or was distracted. Either way, I'm up for a new pump.

It takes forty-eight hours to recalk the old hole, patch the new ones, scrape off the burnt offerings and repaint the hull so the aqua-cops don't get me for being in possession of a shipping hazard, and find a replacement pump. After which I switch on the pink phone. Almost immediately it does its machine-gun *rat-a-tat-tat*.

'I knew you wouldn't show.'

It's the familiar voice with the familiar attitude and the familiar noises in the background.

'The trouble with conclusions, Minnie,' I reply, 'is that people jump to them.'

'You let me down.'

'Everyone gets let down in this world – it's called self-preservation. People never match up to other people's expectations – half the time we don't even match up to our own. But be patient and be there and eventually I'll be there, too.'

'So you're still taking the case?'

'Did I say I wouldn't?'

Harry's in. It doesn't mean his shop's open, just that he's in, the outline of his hunched form barely discernible through the steamed plateglass window. He opens the door but shuts it again immediately I'm inside, the *CLOSED* sign's facing out, and I risk death by saying *Yeah* to a coffee.

'What else do you know about von Franck?' I ask him.

Harry brings a couple of mugs out of the microwave. He stinks of pre-loved nicotine.

'He's king of the developers. If there's an inch of Sydney capable of being built on, you can be sure von Franck's been sniffing around it – the Botanical Gardens, Hyde Park, the airspace over the Harbour Bridge. He makes self-interest look like sacrifice to the ultimate benefit of Sydney when it's just a way of making more money.'

'He sounds smart.'

'He sounds like a greedy bastard, if you ask me.'

'Got anything else?'

Harry tells me that when von Franck arrived in Australia, all he had was his ambition and one Romanian *ban* – the monetary equivalent of a cent – and apparently he's still got it. He came when Sydney was ripe for the plucking and he plucked it. He got into the funeral business and then building – he made influential friends, then he made a motza.

'So he's not popular.'

'Come on, Rainbow, he's a foreigner. On top of which he's successful, and Australians hate success – particularly successful foreigners – unless it's to do with sport. Women fall all over him.'

I look through the steam-fuzzed window at a passing stranger, a black dog, grey clouds in a blue sky.

'Anything else?'

'Not concerning von Franck.'

'They say he killed Cock Robin.'

Harry shrugs.

'Know anyone who might know more?' I ask.

'John Curtis comes to mind.'

'The journo who wrote the piece on the building industry?'

'That's him – the only person who'll give you an opinion on von Franck not laced with arsenic.'

'How come?' I ask.

'Because he's an old-time balanced reporter. I believe there are still some around.'

I cross to the door.

'Thanks, Harry. Also could you get me a list of Cock Robin's enemies?'

'People that hated him enough to kill him? Apart from von Franck, that is?'

I nod, open the steamed-up door, and leave.

Chapter 16

THE PILGARLIC

I find Curtis where you'd expect to find a balanced reporter – propping up the bar in an inner-city pub nursing a bruised ego and a schooner of Old. I know the beer's Old because the sign on the bar says it's on special and I know the scribe's the worse for wear because that's what he's telling the barmaid. I pull out a stool, order a double-sour upside-down and check out my surroundings.

Journalists' drinking holes once made workingmen's pubs look like milk bars. Their most-favoured pastimes being to smoke, drink, curse, fornicate and bash the other bloke senseless before he did it to them. Sometimes they used words but mostly it was fists.

But that was then and this is now. These days, Murdoch's Muckrakers and Fairfax's Flunkies might sound like football teams but they're namby-pamby sweethearts compared with the Hannibals that once hurled typewriters at editors and evil-eyed epithets at everyone else. Now boys and girls come out to play in the quaintly named Dickens Inn, sipping shandies in a non-sexist, smoke-free environment while discussing what they read in the social media, and ping-pong.

I count fifty, most of them wearing earphones

like they're electronic tracking bracelets; spending more time on their techno props than in face-to-face contact; ninety-eight per cent of them staring at tablets, while the remaining two per cent is John Curtis.

'I'm the only journo in town writing without fear or favour. So why do they treat me like shite?' The barmaid's sympathetic, producing a murmured *tut-tut* whenever she manages to get a leg over. 'There are a thousand yarns in this city but does anyone want them? No. And d'ye know why? Because this is Sydney, Australia, and it's up to its neck in corruption. And why? Because of advertising – income stream, money, profits, filthy lucre. What happened to good old-fashioned journalism?' A jerk of a blunt thumb over his shoulder indicates the sewing-circle behind him. '*That lot* happened.'

The scribe's a *pilgarlic* – that's bald, as in *peeled garlic* – shaving his head for reasons best known to himself while also pretending to be drunker than he really is. From the next room comes the *ding-a-ling* of a pokie promising the next spin of the electric wheels is going to be a winner.

I turn back to Curtis.

'What kind of stories?' I ask him.

He gazes at me while I do the same back. He's wearing a red chequerboard shirt and stained jeans; the drunkenness is a front or he'd be off his stool as well as his face; and from the accent he's as Scotch as pot-stilled whisky from Speyside. He doesn't ask: *Who are you?* He's an old-fashioned journalist who knows the best way to get a story is by feigning disinterest. He doesn't ask questions, either; instead he looks drunker than he is and, rather than asking for news, volunteers it.

'Take this Balangalulu project.' He touches the side of his nose with a slab-of-beef hand and winks like he's got the palsy. 'There's more to that than there are pigs in a sty, laddie. Then there's the proposal to develop the Brewster Block – money changed hands on that, too. And the fire in the old Macquarie Barracks the cops say wasn't deliberate. Well, I know better, don't I ...' He takes a swig of his beer but when he puts the glass back on the bar, the level's the same as it was before. 'There's more mischief in the building world than you or I ever dreamed of – or there are stories in a skyscraper ...'

'Tell me about Bluebeard Constructions.'

'You mean von Franck's outfit?' He looks at me suspiciously. 'Why drag him into this?'

I tell him I'm not dragging anyone into anything and he seems to relax.

'It's Blue-*bird* – not Blue*beard* – and von Franck's an exception to the rule: he's straight. My exposés always expect – sorry, ex-*cept* – Ivan and for good reason. He's as clean as the proverbial – the only stories I'll credit about him are good ones, despite what you read in the papers.'

I drain my glass, get the scribe another beer to go with my second, and keep up my side of the pretence. 'It sounds like you've known this *Vladimir* character a long time.'

'It's *Ivan*,' he corrects me; I like it when they do that – it means they're listening. 'And, yeah, I've known him for – hell, it must be going on for thirty years.' He abandons his old drink and picks up the new one and it's my turn to feign disinterest. 'Early in my career I was asked to do a story on immigrants because I was one myself, and Ivan von Franck was one of my stories.'

'Still keep in touch?'

Curtis takes another swig and the level stays the same. 'We're in the same business. Why?'

I shrug. 'I'm a private detective and I hear that he kills people.'

There's a pause – the kind that a person makes before deciding against throwing something and afterwards changes channels. Curtis goes into thinking mode.

'While it's a tough game, I don't think Ivan would kill anyone,' he says at last, taking a swig – and this time the level does change. 'How about you?'

'I don't kill people, either – unless they cross me. But getting back to the hard drive: would you call von Franck a good hater?'

'Why?'

'Like I said – because I hear he kills people.'

'Come on, this is Sydney, Australia and von Franck's a tall poppy.' I've upset the scribe and the lapse back into brogue is the result. 'So, aye, a' course there's aggravation and from plenty a sources but that's *towards* Ivan, not away from him. Take this Cock Robin character, for instance …'

'The joker that was murdered? The union organiser?'

'Union *dis*-organiser more like. Cock Robin set up strikes and took bribes to settle the men, only to immediately foster more dissatisfaction. Over the years he caused von Franck no end of grief, so, *aye* …'

His voice grows careful; von Franck's rich and alive so the libel laws that favour the rich and alive still apply. 'But the coroner didn't finger anyone who might have killed Cock Robin.'

'Do *you* know who killed him?'

Curtis shrugs – or maybe he's just keeping his beer close to his chest. 'I'm a journalist – which means I don't pay attention to rumours.'

'Given that Cock Robin's dead, who does von Franck get aggravation from now?'

'You say you're a private detective ...'

I nod and hand him a card – the one where *BERT SMITH'S MATRIMONIAL INVESTIGATIONS* is crossed out and *JOHN JONES, SPECIALIST IN MISSING PERSONS* inserted in its place.

'... In which case, you'd have a story or two you could put my way' – he checks the card – 'Johnnie ...'

'I might do,' I say. 'Meanwhile, you were saying no-one actively dislikes von Franck – what about the other way round?'

'You mean who *likes* him?'

'No – I mean, who does von Franck actively hate.'

'Clean Fill.'

'*Clean Fill*? The stuff that builders put in holes in the ground?'

He allows himself the shadow of a smile. 'Aye, that's the essence of the name – if you Australians are clever about anything other than sport, it's names. It must be because you're antipodeans but most nicknames are upside down. *Clean Fill* – real name, Phillip McLean O'Hare – is anything but unblemished.'

'You sure got a way with words, Curtis.'

He laughs – I've made him happy. 'Nicknames are *bynames*, *hypocoristic*, *cognomens*, *pen-names*, *pseudonyms* and *briquets* – I particularly like *briquets* because it sounds like *brickbats*.'

I've fed his ego. I down the rest of my sour and place the empty on the counter.

'So what's he do, this Clean Fill joker?'

'You must live under a rock, Johnnie-boy. Clean Fill was once a shyster – that is, a crooked lawyer.'

'What does he do now?'

'The general populace. He's a crooked politician – the Minister for Development.'

'Where would I find him?'

'Down by the seaside – in white man's country.' Curtis smiles; it's an interesting smile – full of bonhomie but at the same time guarded; he touches the side of his nose again. 'So come on, now it's your turn – what d'ye have for me?'

'I'll put my mind to it,' I promise.

That's when he asks who I really am and who I work for and I tell him the answer to the first question's *Bob Brown* and to the second, the general good. After which I straighten my fedora, climb down off the stool and make my way out of the pub to breathe once more the foetid air of the city.

Chapter 17

TWO-BIT CHARMER

Flea: *a wingless, bloodsucking insect of the order
Siphonaptera, a parasite of man and other mam-
mals which – by sucking the blood of rats and then
of humans – is capable of spreading disease ...*

As soon as I'm aware of their presence – there's a
shadow between me and the deep-blue nausea and
another by the *Vincentia* – I haul out the Smith &
Double-Yew and take refuge behind the burnt-out
wreck that was once a Toyota Corolla. The Good
Book says: *There's a time to be born and a time to
die; a time to kill and a time to heal; a time to stand
and deliver and a time to duck for cover.* I do like the
Good Book says and stay behind the Corolla.

My mind's on holiday or they wouldn't have got
me. I was too busy brooding. There's two of them –
one tall, the other short – and they're onto me before
I know it.

Crooks take stuff that isn't theirs – cars, CD
players, reputations, a life. In Sydney they're like
fleas on a dog and I'm the dog that every second flea
in Sydney wants a bite of. I'm wearing the sunset-red
jacket and it makes me a sitting duck for whoever
wants to take a pot at me. Which might be Pandora,
the cops, a random player, or someone completely
new to the game – like the two jokers who have just

offloaded themselves from the Reserves bench and into my life.

I go into a whirlygig from the ballet *Petrushka* – half of it by intent, the rest by chance – but these two know their business, and the kick to the side of my skull is by the book while the thump in the ribs isn't for medicinal purposes. I go down and see the rest of the world go by – a dame in Givenchy; a pack of schoolkids; and a couple of surf heroes. None of whom stop because clearly I deserve it. The tall one's boot comes for my face. I avoid a direct hit but it grazes the side of my head and my left ear starts playing *Waltzing Matilda* – the version with the didgeridoo improvisation as background and the side drums in the refrain.

It must be the surprise element but the old dame wielding the umbrella appearing like Boadicea on a winning streak sends the tall thug into the camellias while the smaller one reassesses his priorities. I manage to find my feet – it's not easy when I don't know where they are – and my head feels like it's been taken off and not put back on straight again. A cop appears, the small thug helps the big thug out of the bushes and they disappear.

'You from around here?' the cop asks. I shake my head; I'm trying to change tracks; I've never liked didgeridoos; the cop takes it as a *No*. 'Then get the hell out of my beautiful, idyllic suburb and take your problems with you,' he adds, dispersing onlookers while I make my own arrangements. Which don't involve leaving.

It's like they haven't changed the use of the joint so much as updated the menu, a fish-and-chips sign still visible under the palimpsest on the sea-rusted awning reading: *ELECTORAL OFFICE OF PHILLIP McLEAN O'HARE*. The door's got a red waratah painted on it to prove this is NSW and opens onto a big room containing a counter and a dame sitting behind it.

'Why, hello!' she says like we're married but haven't had our first argument yet. 'What happened to your face?'

'I fell by the wayside.'

She looks nonplussed. 'What can I do for you?'

'I'm after the incumbent.'

'The what?'

'Is your father in?'

'Do you mean the Minister?'

I'm trying to turn off the recording; I can still hear the didgeridoos. Her look takes in the battered hat, rearranged coat and smacked-together features — after which she reaches under the counter like she's been taught when confronted by people like me.

'Do you have an appointment?' she asks.

'I don't need one — I'm a constituent.'

'A what?'

'A member of the electorate, an ordinary Joe, a voter: one of the people who put your father where he is.'

'Oh, one of those!'

She changes her mind about the button and a voice emerges because she's got the *Telefunken* on *Loudspeaker* when the dialogue should just be between her and her progenitor.

'I thought I told you to hold all calls, Molly.'

'But it's not a call, Daddy, it's one of those what-do-you-call-them – *persistents*.'

Sigh from the other end of the phone. Then, 'Did he give a name?'

The dame puts a hand over the receiver like she's seen it done in the movies. 'What's your name?' she whispers.

'Mr Jones.'

She takes her mitt off the phone. 'It's a Mr Smith.'

Sigh from the speaker; the voice softens – she can't help being what she is. 'Very well, tell him I can give him five minutes and send him in.'

He's not what I expect but they rarely are. I pictured him as a broad-shouldered brute but instead he's a two-bit charmer in a two-bit charmer's suit with a face like a dummy: small build, narrow shoulders, close-together eyes, and the proud possessor of the family squint. Talking of *two-bit*: something glimmers on the floor – I place a foot over it as I take a seat.

'Don't worry about the girl,' he says. 'She means well. She just let two others in she shouldn't have and I roused on her for it, so she's a bit twitchy.' The squint settles in for the long haul as he examines what's left of my face. 'Do I know you?'

'No. But you know Ivan von Franck.'

An expression darts across his face like a frightened rabbit, before disappearing back into its warren. 'Are you telling me Ivan sent you?'

'I'm not telling you anything except that I need to know something.'

'What's this all about?'

I hand him a card – the one that says I'm Simon Templar and I'm a saint. 'I'm a journalist doing stories on important people.' All right, so the idea was inspired by Curtis. 'I'll be getting around to you before long but at the moment I'm doing a piece on von Franck.'

Chapter 18

THE CAT THAT BARKED

He looks up from the card. 'It says here *Without Flair or Flavour.* What the hell does that mean?'

It was a phrase Curtis used – before the machine on the railway station spat out the card and before the misprint; it sounded good at the time but doesn't bear scrutiny now.

'It means I'm not afraid of the truth.'

'Who *is* afraid of the truth!' Clean Fill tries for a grin but it only accentuates the family resemblance. 'That was a joke, Mr Templar. So tell me: who do you tell the truth for – who's your employer?'

'I haven't got one, I freelance.'

'Which means you've been sacked by all the major players and now work for some two-bit street rag promoting some social issue or other, produced on a Romeo-machine somewhere in downtown Chippendale.' He flips the card like he knows where it's from. 'All right, on the off-chance that – as well as being unemployed – you're also a constituent, and therefore possess a vote, I'll allow you five questions. But first: why me?'

'Because you know von Franck and also because you're the relevant Minister.'

'So what's your first question?'

'What's he like?'

'He's a top guy.'

'Why do you say that?'

'Because of the laws of libel.'

'So you're afraid what you *really* want to say might land you in trouble?'

'I didn't say that.'

'All right – you're the Development Minister and von Franck's a builder. Did von Franck donate to your slush fund and afterwards demand favours – or issue threats if the favours didn't happen?'

'No comment.' He shuffles some papers. 'Okay, that's it – you've asked your five questions.'

'One was for clarification.'

'All right, I'll allow one more.'

'Going back to the *fear* thing, what are you afraid of? The law of libel – or the law according to von Franck?'

'That's two questions and my answer's *No comment* to both.' He presses down on the desk and raises himself like a crane on a building site. 'Now if you've got any more questions you can put them in writing.'

'I also want to ask about Robin Fahey – Cock Robin.'

'Why – is he unemployed, too?'

I reach down like I'm tying my whitesides and when I straighten the shiny thing on the floor has made its way into my pocket. I'm a bowerbird for facts and this is a fact.

'Cock Robin's dead.'

Unlike the dud hand Minnie dealt the court, the second address works. It's a pretty little joint in inner-city Camperdown – she must have rung from the airport just to throw me – with too many coloured windows, too much pink paint and a bunch of knives that jangle at a touch. When she throws open the door she's clutching a gizmo with a flashing light on it and she's not happy.

'For God's sake shut up, I've just put Fiona down!'

I follow her inside past a phone table with a picture of a man, a woman and a baby on it; a set of stairs; through a living room containing too many flowers; and end up in a ploughed field containing a garden chair, a clothesline full of nappies, a stump and a shed with a gate beside it. The dame sits on the chair, leaving me in charge of the stump.

'I see you use real nappies,' I say, to break the ice.

'I do it for the environment. But we're not here to talk about the environment.'

'So why are we here?'

She shrugs. 'I suppose asking you to take on this case seemed like a good idea at the time. I tracked you to your boat in the belief that whoever had that pink phone killed my husband. Only to find that you were nothing more than a detective with a dead man's phone.' She shrugs. 'I thought you could help but I see I was wrong.'

I climb down off the stump. 'I'll let myself out.'

'He was such a bastard!'

'*He* being your late husband Cock Robin, the joker in the picture in the hall?'

Smiling for the camera but still nasty-looking. I wait and after a while the dame continues.

'He was a thug who went out of his way to hurt people – especially me.' She touches her nose. 'For years I put up with his violence thinking it was normal. I actually thought I was lucky because I had a man.' She shakes her head. 'I thought parenthood might change him but it only made him worse. One night he shook Fiona and when – when he did that I – all right, yes: I wanted to kill him.'

I get myself back on the stump. 'So did you?'

She nods her head and shakes it all at the same time. 'That's exactly what the police – specifically Detective-Sergeant Richard bloody Richardson – decided when they found Cock Robin's body. I actually heard one of them say: *Nine times out of ten it's the wife.* But how could it have been me when I thought you did it?'

'Look – I'm sorry, what's your real name?'

'Maxine – Maxine Grant.'

'Okay, Minnie or Maxi or whoever the hell you are – the kind of logic you just used says that if a cat thinks it's a dog it must bark. But let's take a Jail Pass on the logic and stick to the questions: where did the killing take place, what was the cause of death and did they ever find the murder weapon?' Court transcripts can be misleading – deliberately or otherwise. 'And I need to hear it from you, even though I've read the transcript. So tell me about the murder.'

Chapter 19

SUCKLING BABES
TELL NO TALES

The gizmo in the dame's lap burps and farts and starts chattering; at first I think it's talkback radio until I realise it's a back-to-base alarm and the kid's hungry. The squawking fades and the dame manages to focus.

'The killing was done with what the police called a *blunt instrument*. They never found the murder weapon even though a lot of men in blue singlets spent several days digging up my backyard.' Hence the potato field. 'They found his body over there.' She shudders as she waves towards the shed. 'When I came downstairs and saw his body, a great wave of sadness washed over me, when I should have been relieved he was gone.'

'You mean you were actually on the premises when Cock Robin copped it?'

Minnie nods. 'I was upstairs feeding Fiona.'

I raise my voice to be heard over the racket coming out of the gizmo. 'Did you happen to *hear* anything?'

The dame shakes her head – the noise has risen to a crescendo but she still wants to answer the question. 'As I said, I was feeding Fiona. There could have been a world war for all I knew.'

'Not much of an alibi, is it? I mean you could hardly get little Fiona to swear she was using you as a milkbar when her father was murdered. You could have come down, whacked your husband over the head when he wasn't looking, disposed of the murder weapon, gone back upstairs and finished feeding the kid – all before dialling 000.' I glance at her. 'I assume you called Emergency?'

She nods wanly. 'You think the same as them, don't you? But I tell you I didn't do it. And I can't say I wouldn't have asked you to take the case if I was innocent because you'd just say ...'

Whatever argument she's got wouldn't stand up in a court of law, which means she was lucky she didn't stand up in a real one – only a coronial inquiry. But the question remains: why wasn't she charged? She answers without being asked.

'The long and the short of it was that Detective-Sergeant Richardson couldn't take his eyes off me. And all his questions steered me away from culpability. *You loved him, didn't you?* he asked. *You're not a strong woman, physically, are you? You heard a noise as of someone entering the house while you were upstairs and when you came down to investigate ...*

'All his questions were like that; he put words in my mouth. I suppose a lawyer might call Richardson's questions *leading*. And because I was scared, I let myself be led.'

'And where did he lead you?'

'Not into his bed, if that's what you mean. That's what he wanted to happen, of course. A woman knows these things.'

'But you must have been grateful that he got you off the hook …'

'Yeah. Off one hook and onto another – off a murder charge and onto Sergeant bloody Richardson's *Most Wanted* list. I felt like a – a fish that takes a bait when it thinks it's being thrown a lifeline. He *wanted* me obligated so I became obligated. It didn't mean I had to *oblige* him. Not in that way, anyway.'

'So what did you do?'

'I said *No*, of course – except that Richardson wouldn't accept *No*. He seemed to think I was playing hard to get. The fact I'd put up with my husband for so long somehow worked against me – Richardson thought he was Mr Wonderful by comparison.' She shrugs. 'He's a very persistent man. You saw the flowers in the living room – pots and pots of them? Well, they're from him. It's as if he thinks I'm an epitaph on a headstone he can wear down if he *thrusts* at me enough. And behind all his thrusting is the very real threat I'll end up convicted of a murder I didn't commit if I don't – and where would Fiona be then? Robin warned me police can plant evidence proving beyond reasonable doubt that someone did something they didn't. And it wouldn't be double jeopardy because I was never tried, was I? Besides, Richardson really does seem to think I'm guilty …'

'Which is why you want me to prove you're not.'

The kid's screams are close to Force 9 on the Bo-diddly scale and the waves are starting to turn into spindrift. Minnie gets up.

'Will you try to prove my innocence or not? I

know you know I didn't do it, which means it must have been von Franck. When he was in the witness box saying how he much he admired my husband, I *knew* he could kill his own mother. Anyway, I need to feed Fiona.' As she disappears inside she calls over her shoulder, 'Can you wait till I come back?'

Workshops are like mausoleums and the shed at the end of Minnie's garden is no exception. Light creeps through a window like a burglar, cobwebs dangle from rafters, and sawdust hangs off the cobwebs. Electrical tools are lined up like an identity parade while a grease-stained workbench squats under a shadow board. Before he became a corpse, Cock Robin was a do-it-yourselfer.

I push back the hat, pull out the torch and send its beam for a stroll among the cobwebs. Rusty pipes lie on the rafters; sky glimmers through holes in the roof; and the bin contains offcuts. The workbench is cluttered and a tool's missing from the shadow board.

They call them shadow boards because the shapes of the tools drawn on them look like shadows. And this particular shadow says what's missing is a 24-inch Blackbird Carrington monkey wrench weighing in the vicinity of five pounds – more than enough to qualify as the kind of blunt instrument that can kill someone. If Richardson had organised a proper search – instead of getting his glorified gravediggers simply to plough up the yard – he might have found what he was meant to be looking for. Only he didn't find it because he wasn't looking – hence all the flowers.

'Where are you?'

I'd forgotten nursing mothers do it in public now and that's what Skinny Minnie's doing. I dowse the torch, step across to the shadow board, select a short-handled sledgehammer that would weigh about the same as the wrench, belt a nail halfway into an offcut, and head back outside.

I hold up the block of wood. 'Could you finish hammering this nail in for me?' I ask.

Minnie frowns. 'Why?'

'Call it a whim. I'll hold Philomena.'

The dame can't swing the hammer – even when she holds it near the head – and I'm experiencing much the same problem with the kid. We do the swap back. Minnie didn't kill her husband.

Chapter 20

VOICES IN THE HALL

She's gone back to feeding the kid so I heft the hammer. 'A couple more questions. The first being: who else, apart from von Franck, had it in for your husband?'

'A lot of people, because he was so nasty.'

'Enough to kill him?'

'That's different. To do that, you'd need to be a particular kind of person. Plus there'd have to be a particular reason to do it.'

'Not necessarily – having a bad temper would be enough. But putting those two factors together – the right person and a sufficient motive – can you think of anyone?'

Minnie shakes her head. 'No-one – apart from von Franck. And if people don't just kill people, then I suppose intense dislike wouldn't be enough … ?'

'So why do you think it was von Franck?'

Just then, the knives on the front verandah make the same kind of noise they made when I hit them.

'You expecting anyone?' I ask her.

She shakes her head. 'I never have visitors apart from …' She frowns and her eyes get that scared look. 'It must be him.'

'Okay. He's just a man in a uniform, a public servant that happens to carry a gat.' The words ring as hollow as the cutlery chimes; I keep talking; sometimes there's nothing else to keep. 'Cops might be cops but they're still no more than cops. Just act normal. Tell him I'm your brother, John Peel, and all you got to say then is goodbye.'

I park the hammer and take the babe – she's got her hands full without having a built-in diner. The babe arches its back and screams as the dame pads past the pots of flowers, down the hallway and opens the door. I bounce the babe like I've seen it done on television but the babe still howls.

'You took your bloody time,' says the visitor.

'I'm … sorry, but my – brother's here.'

The babe strains in my arms and there's a rush of activity in its nether regions followed by a stench you could grow roses on. The kid relaxes. I've got the magic touch. Voices in the hall.

'Your husband's not even cold yet,' Richardson is saying, 'and you've already got lovers crawling all over you.'

'It's my brother.'

'So I'll just come and meet him. By the way, I brought you something.'

The two sets of footsteps advance up the hall – her bare ones and his booted ones – and when she appears she's clutching yet another flowerpot while the bull's staring at me like it's only a matter of time before he makes the arrest. He's short, maybe five-ten, but he's built of much the same material they make grenades from. His smile's annealed steel and the eyes could blow up a safe.

'Ah, the baby minder,' he says softly.

There's no number on his chest because he's not

wearing a uniform. But he's still a bent cop from the soles of his shiny black boots to the top of his frizz-cut hair.

'What's the matter – cat got your tongue?'

'I'm Minnie's brother, John Peel.'

Chapter 21

WHEN THE MUSIC STOPS

He narrows his eyes until all that's left is slits. 'As in: *D'ye ken John Peel with his coat so gay?* Yeah, it figures.' Richardson turns back to the dame like I'm expected to know who he is. Rhomboids, deltoids and triceps ripple under his coat as he hunches his shoulders, feet wide apart like he thinks he's bigger than he is. 'New evidence has come to light.' It's like I'm not here. 'The result of some over-keen constable sticking in his bib where it's not wanted. Turns out that your DNA's all over the –'

'But I tell you I had nothing to do with it!'

'Then you've got nothing to worry about, have you, my pretty?' His rough voice turns smooth as he shrugs his shoulders. 'But if you ever *are* worried, you've only got to say the word and I'll come running.' The dame's gripping the flowerpot like the blooms aren't roses but belladonna. 'Mind you water those flowers or they'll die – everything dies.' Richardson turns so he's facing me again but this time he's up-close and personal. 'Do I know you from somewhere, Peel?'

'I don't know,' I reply. 'Do you?'

He holds out his right hand. 'Show me your licence, smart guy.'

'I don't drive.'

He flicks his fingers. 'Some other ID then – Medicare card, library ticket or life membership of the Phantom Club.'

'I don't get sick and I don't read.'

'You telling me you've got no ID?'

I don't tell him I don't exist. Tell him I don't exist and he's got the arrest he wants while I get the arrest that I don't. The dame steps between us.

'My brother's helping with the grieving process.'

Richardson lowers his fist. 'Is that what they call it now? The way I see it, you're only too happy to be shot of your husband so you can play up. So happy, in fact, that people might be excused for thinking you knocked him off.'

'But you know that I didn't!'

That's when he turns on her and that's when the dame looks scared all over again.

'That's the funny thing about the law – it can find people guilty when they're innocent or innocent when they're guilty. Criminality's a moveable feast, with guilt reliant on the rules applying at the time. The trick is to make sure the rules don't apply to you when the music stops. Think about that while you're grieving.' He prods my chest; I don't like jokers that prod my chest; but I already don't like this joker. 'I've got the strongest feeling we're going to meet again, Phantom Man.' He indicates the dame with a nod of his steel-wool head. 'In fact, I wouldn't be surprised if you're still around when I return to arrest Little Miss Innocent.'

'I'm so glad you were here,' Minnie breathes once Richardson's gone. 'He'll be back, though. What am I going to do?'

'You got any friends, Minnie?'

She pats the babe. 'Cock Robin was a control freak. I wasn't allowed to talk to another man and it was pretty much the same with women – he felt threatened by everyone.'

'There must be someone.'

'I suppose there could be one person …'

'Who?'

Minnie takes a deep breath. 'Her name's – Tsunami.'

'Are you sure of the address?'

We're in the bush – in Sydney the wilderness starts as soon as the money runs out – in the kind of place where killers dump corpses knowing that only lost people end up here, never to be seen again. The cabbie dumped us at a sign reading *NO ADMITTANCE* and left as soon as I paid. It was a seventy-buck ride but he didn't stay to give me the change from a C-note. The light from the sickle moon's fighting a losing battle with the clouds while the leaf canopy takes care of the rest.

'There never was an address as such …'

'So walk me through it again.'

'As I said, Cock Robin didn't allow me to …'

The bush noises are the sounds of nightmares – the sharps and shreds of untuned violas, rustlings in the undergrowth, the flapping of wings that could be the etiolated skins of dead men, and the rush of unseen creatures fleeing the bloodstained claws of Doom.

'The technology he installed in my mobile was the same as that used for tracker bracelets.' The babe starts whimpering again, its *tremolo* at one with the rest of the bush. 'There was no way I could maintain a proper friendship – much less an improper one. Robin used to go through my call log.'

I look at the bush. No-one's home. There's not even a home for anyone to be home in.

'This *acquaintance* of yours – would you describe her as a friend?'

'I don't know all that much about her. You asked for a name and hers was the only one that came to mind.'

'Except you didn't give a name. Tsunami's not a name – it's a death-defying leap into the unknown, a natural phenomenon that kills people.'

Chapter 22

THE VOICE IN AISLE 16

'Her real name's Sue Mahoney but it sounds like *Tsunami* so that's what I call her. She'd come around and we'd have tea and talk. One day Robin arrived home unexpectedly and – it was weird – looked taken aback when he saw Tsunami. I thought there'd be fireworks but I was wrong. Tsunami had been coming around for a few weeks before he saw her and – he, well, after that, he stopped hitting me. But while Tsunami would come to my place, I never went to hers: he wouldn't let me.'

'So as far as you knew, Tsunami lived in a hole in the ground.' We've got to move but when we do it's got to be in the right direction or we'll join all the other corpses in the forest. 'How did you meet?'

'I had little freedom but of course we had to eat so Robin let me go to the supermarket and that's where I met her. She was a voice in Aisle 16. I was reaching up for a box of breakfast cereal when I heard someone say: *Don't touch that crap, it'll kill you!* It was like the shelf talking. I went, *Who's that?* And Tsunami appeared.'

'Did you consider the possibility she might have been lying in wait?'

'Why would she do that? No, our meeting was accidental: we were two lost souls in a supermarket.'

'How did she strike you, this fellow lost soul?'

'It was – strange. It was like being with a man but without the tension. I've forgotten what we talked about but it seemed as if she was – well, flirting. She was – handsome, in a way. She had a strong personality while I'm more maternal. So, yes, she was mannish, both physically and in the way she dressed. That first time she wore men's trousers and a man's shirt, her hair was cropped short, and she had no make-up on. She just stood in the breakfast section with her feet apart.'

'Did she tell you anything about herself – like what she did for a living?'

'We didn't talk about anything in particular and what we did talk about I've forgotten. But I committed the directions she gave me to memory because I knew I might be in need of a bolt hole one day: *Take the Workhorse Parkway, turn off at so many clicks, you'll see a fire trail, go another so many clicks, then head north, and after half an hour switch to north by north-east ...*'

'Does she walk fast?'

'Like a gazelle.'

I check the watch with the compass in it I got from Goldilocks at the Morgue and do the calculations. If Minnie's memory's good we're twenty minutes from our destination.

'Any hint of a profession?' I ask as I bash through the undergrowth. 'A surgical smell that might suggest *nurse*? The physique of a dancer or the translucent pallor of a nun?'

'She smelled of cement.' Minnie pulls a twig out of her hair. 'I met an abattoir worker once and knew immediately what he did for a living, due to the smell of – it was a sort of *barbecue* smell. Well, Tsunami had a *cement* smell.'

I put two and two together and don't like what I come up with. I've got a lot of questions but I don't ask them. Instead I recheck the compass and head north by north-east and the dame follows.

'Where are we going?'

'North by north-east.'

Through the trees I make out a small block-shaped affair, little more than a box on wheels. It's painted dark but I can't determine the colour, only that the caravan sucks in light like a black hole. A small set of steps sticks out from under the door and a yellow light gleams from a small window set high in the side. The ground around it has been cleared but there are still a few trees. By the window light I note the overhead branches have been stripped away. Whoever lives here knows their bushcraft. Probably eats berries, roots and leaves …

'Are we there yet?' Minnie asks.

I hold out an arm and hit soft.

'Stop!'

It's old fashioned in these times of lasers but it's still effective and if I hadn't been looking I wouldn't have noticed because the trip cord's completely buried, except for where a wombat, a bush turkey, a fox or a feral cat unearthed it: an innocent-looking wire that must go right around the clearing. I motion to the dame to stand still.

'This would form concentric circles an irregular distance apart.' I put down Minnie's suitcase, kneel and scratch at the dirt around the wire. 'They'll be connected to a battery which would power an alarm. The system would be so sensitive the slightest touch would activate it …'

Chapter 23

A CASE OF MISTAKEN IDENTITY

I've never met Pandora, I don't even remember when or where I first heard the name, or if the name's imagined or real. But for as long as I can remember, the deadly and significant *idea* of Pandora has been lodged in my mind.

I spent my first five years on the funny farm — that's what we used to call the hippy commune in the north of NSW — it was a loony bin, a madhouse, Bedlam, in which the smell of dope eclipsed the scent of eucalypt.

The adults — I realised in my own adulthood — were always half-stoned and forever in and out of each other's wigwams. Half the time we didn't know if we were Arthur or Martha or even who our parents were. I could have been spawned by a wombat. Then one night with the sky ablaze with scorpions my mother immolated herself. She was high on a burning windmill and even higher on dope and she took my little sister with her screaming into the night. I was five at the time and scared and hid behind a totem pole. I can still see its Easter Island face with its grinning lips and flattened nose, the three great scars on each of its cheeks angled upwards. But most of all I remember its eyes because there weren't any – just two empty holes in the gleaming white carapace of the skull.

That was the night Pandora entered my life. Since then, I've often seen her, half-hidden behind buildings, a vehicle or a tree. I've sensed her evil, tried to apply logic to her and failed. I grew up knowing she could be around the next corner. It helped me survive. Because I knew if I relaxed for a moment, Pandora would get me, so I never relaxed. No logic to it, I just – knew.

I've left Minnie-Ha-Ha, the babe and the suitcase and I'm halfway up the steps to the caravan. The gat's shelved because we're not in enemy territory and the clouds have parted company with the moon, turning the trees and caravan silver. My knocking echoes on emptiness like I'm banging on a bongo. There's no sound from inside, just the pale light from the window and the whispers of the bush and I'm starting to think it's going to be a long walk back to town.

I'm concentrating on the van. My weight makes the springs creak but – apart from the echoes of my knocking and the sounds of the bush – it's all I can hear. On the boat there's always the familiar fart-gurgle of the water, but here it's different – the whisper of the wind, the rustle of land animals and the hoot of an owl. Familiar sounds if you're familiar with them but I'm not.

My first thought is for Minnie and the babe.

They're a long way back and exposed. Death moves quiet in the bush, no more than a shadow on the periphery of your consciousness, until suddenly you're no longer alive.

I don't know how I become aware of the danger because there's no noise: it's – just – something – visceral. It could be a movement of the clouds, a shift in light intensity, the flicker from silver to –

Or it could be my febrile imagination. Because when I look back, Minnie is still there, a moon-glossed figure hugging her babe while – a short distance away from her – the suitcase looms large on the ground. Except that –

At first I don't notice because my attention's on the dame and the babe. They've become one, a solitary shape in the moonlight, their shadow seemingly more substantial than they are. From the vantage point of the steps, I quarter the area. My footprints are stones in amber and sticks lie stark among the leaves while the place where I rooted out the trip wire looks like snout marks made by a boar. The bag moves.

Your eyes do that – suggest movement where none exists. But while such phenomena are common at sea, in the bush they're –

The suitcase *moved*. It wasn't much of a movement but it moved. In the normal course of events bags don't move – unless someone moves them. Or unless they're not bags at all.

That's when I see that the black shape – what I *thought* was a suitcase – isn't a case at all but ...

Almost as though it *senses* that I know, the shape moves, lengthens and becomes –

I've never seen Pandora – only her outline, her shadow, the *idea* of her – but I know what she looks like. She's a figure in a black – a *female* figure in black – lithe and dangerous, with an ill-defined face and carrying a knife. She wears figure-hugging clothes – the one garment stretched thin, like a second skin, black. And that's what rises before me now, a figure in black with a knife and Minnie and her babe between us – all of them bathed in the snow-white light of the moon.

I'm quick but the figure's quicker, feinting to the right before diving the other way and I hear the *whang!* of a knife as it nails my fedora to the van. And when I look again, the figure's already got another knife in its hand. I hurl myself down the steps. The knife will go through my chest or pierce an eye but the dame and the babe will survive, I try to reassure myself, because I'm the one that Pandora's after …

I awaken cushioned in lava, blinking upwards, to see a curved ceiling and below it the face of a concerned Minnie. I'm dead and in heaven. Except that Rube always said that there wasn't a heaven and Rube only ever dealt in facts.

'You're alive,' the angel murmurs.

My head hurts and when I try to raise it, it hurts

even more. 'Pandora …' I murmur.

The van's the usual home-away-from-home – a crumpled mattress, sink, fridge, stove, bench, table, and not nearly enough air. Minnie's shaking her head.

'What is it with this Pandora? While you were out to it she was all you could talk about. And now you're awake you're still talking about her. Who the hell is she?'

'Where's Pandora?'

'There you go again,' Minnie says, bewildered. 'Who?'

That's when I realise that the apparition with the knives only *looked* like Pandora – looked like Pandora, dressed like Pandora, acted like Pandora and nearly killed me like Pandora might one day kill me. I shake my head – to clear it but also because I'm confused.

'The dame in black – the one that tried to kill me …'

It's Minnie's turn to shake her head.

'I presume you mean *Tsunami*. She heard us coming and when she saw you she threw the knife. After that she knocked you out with a kick to the head. Then I called out and … Anyway, she's gone for a walk – she said she needed a bit of space to think. Look, I'm grateful, Mr Peel, or whoever you are, but …'

My hat's on the table and there's a hole in it and the dame's *grateful*?

She shrugs.

'Tsunami acted in self-defence. She didn't mean to kill you. In fact, she aimed to miss.'

'Did you know she could handle knives before she aimed to miss?'

'Well, no, actually, but I … she –'

The door flings open and there's Tsunami. She doesn't look happy. She looks dangerous, menacing and beautiful, but not happy, and her words suit her looks.

'I've thought it through.' She's looking at Minnie, not at me. 'Cock Robin's dead and his murder survived the cops, an autopsy and the coroner. You're in the clear, Minnie. So why come here? And why' – a jerk of a thumb in my direction – 'bring him with you?'

'Because of the cops in general and one in particular.'

'What cops in general and which one in particular?'

The babe's on the bed, grumbling but asleep. Minnie tells Tsunami about the cops in general and Sergeant Richardson in particular and while she's talking I check out the dame who almost killed me.

Chapter 24

WHO KILLED COCK ROBIN?

There's something disturbing about her, like she has two parts and neither of them fits. She's strong but she's also ephemeral as if – like the wave that Minnie named her after – she could destroy everything in her path but afterwards become nothing. She has dark hair cropped short, black eyes, mobile lips, sinuous body and intelligent eyes ...

'So while this big, brave detective is working out who killed Cock Robin, you need a refuge from a cop, is that what you're telling me?' she asks Minnie.

'It would only be me and Fiona.'

'And what happens *after* I give you refuge, Minnie? Do you move on or move in? And if it's the latter, long are we talking?'

'Please, just until Mr Peel finds the murderer. I know Richardson will never give up as long as he thinks there's a chance of getting me into bed and that will be for as long as he can frame me. He won't rest until either I give in or we find the killer. I – thought I could stay at your place.' Minnie looks around dubiously. 'But there's not enough room, is there? How was I to know you lived in the bush like a wild animal ... ?'

Tsunami examines a bootee. 'Don't worry, I'm not turning you out, sweetie. I happen to like my privacy but I have another home.'

'You mean a proper home?'

'I only come here when things get too much for me. I gave you directions to the van without really thinking you might try and find me.' She shrugs. 'You can stay at the other place – but only on one condition.'

It was my hat she nailed. I've got a right to butt in. 'What's the condition?' I say.

It's the first time she's looked at me since she threw the knife.

'That I'm going to help you find Robbie's killer,' she replies.

'Why would you want to do that?'

'Let's just say I have a vested interest.' She nods at the dame. 'I saw what Robbie did to her and I can guess what the cop could do by way of a follow-up. Isn't that enough reason?'

Yeah, it's *enough* reason but I don't know if it's the *right* reason. But in the end there's no option but to agree because I need to park the dame while I get on with the job.

Balmain's a poodle stretched out in the sun, its paws in the water. Tsunami's home away from home is a picturesque little joint overlooking a picturesque bay with a picturesque ex-oil refinery in it and Minnie's standing in the doorway like she's waving her boyfriend off to war – except that there are two of us, and one's a dame.

We're in a pub – Tsunami's idea – and we're nursing a couple of triple-strength rums – my idea. Tsunami could be a bloke, perched on her stool with her trouser-clad legs so far apart she might be trying to split the atom. I prefer to operate alone but I need to know what her game is – if she's in love with Minnie or killed Cock Robin or both. My money's on both, only I don't tell her that. I want her where I can find her and if I tell her what I think, I won't see her for the dust.

'What's your real name?' she asks.

'Brown.'

'So what do you know, Brown?'

When I tell her I know that the prime suspect's von Franck, the arched eyebrows in the beautiful face become even more arched. 'You don't mean *the* von Franck?'

'How many are there?' I finish my rum, catch the eye of the barmaid with the cherubic lips and order two more. The pub reeks of perfume, sweat, garlic and – nearer at hand – a cement smell. I ask the question.

'You in the building game, Tsunami?'

'I'm a vet.'

'You mean you look after *animals*?'

Tsunami shakes her head. 'Haven't you noticed all the scars, Mr Brown – together with the way I talk and my *attitude*? Plus the fact that I can afford a nice home in an even nicer suburb due to an interest-free loan, yet prefer to live in a caravan? And what about that hole I put in your hat?' She shrugs. 'Forget animals, I'm a *veteran*-type vet – ex-Major Susan Mahoney, Australian Engineers – skilled in the martial arts as well as in engineering. Someone who served in one war too many and can't forget it; seen too many deaths and can't forget them, either; and craves excitement because she's reached the point where she can't live without it.'

'Is that why you want to hunt down a killer?'

'It's one reason.'

'Last time I looked, being a vet wasn't a full-time profession. You're young, bright and attractive, so why not do something useful?'

She laughs her deep laugh and somehow it's no longer masculine. 'As well as being a war vet I'm also a civil engineer. It's why I was in the army – I build bridges. And before you ask – *civil* in this context doesn't mean I'm not a criminal or polite. It just means that I know my way around buildings – what holds them up and what lets them down.'

'You've got some connection to Cock Robin. What are you – an ex-wife?'

'Cock Robin was a cock-of-the-walk, a bully and a toad. When I first met Minnie, she told me how she came by her injuries, and my soldiering instincts told me to go in.' She realises she might have said something she didn't mean to. 'That is, I felt I had to help her.'

'By bumping off Cock Robin?'

'*Who killed Cock Robin?*' she quotes, because sooner or later someone had to. '*I, said the Sparrow, with my bow and arrow, I killed Cock Robin.*' She downs the rest of her drink and clicks her fingers for more without checking if the barmaid's looking; because she knows she is – just like she knows more about Cock Robin than she's letting on. 'I'm sorry to disappoint you, soldier, but unless you haven't noticed, I'm no sparrow.'

Chapter 25

I, SAID THE SPARROW

I've got three suspects now – Skinny Minnie, von Franck and Tsunami – and I've met the first and the last and there's still one to go. But when we turn up at the site of von Franck's latest and greatest skyscraper, a familiar-looking gorilla wearing a hard hat and an even harder expression tells us the boss is too busy to see anyone. Tsunami shrugs and bends to peer through a hole in the wraparound hoarding marked *FOR THE FOOTPATH SUPERINTENDENT* while I occupy the hole next door. The structure's a concrete skeleton rearing from a giant's grave.

'Like boys the world over,' Tsunami murmurs, 'von Franck's got to have a bigger car, a bigger cannon, a bigger cockle-doodle-doo. This thing's 300 metres high – a thousand bloody *feet* – nearly as tall as the Sydney Tower and more than twice the height of the Bridge. A thousand apartments and not nearly enough parking places, because von Franck's bought someone off. Average price of units when they're finished: $2 million. Twelve lifts. And views to die for. It's so big, von Franck had to get clearance from Sydney Airport to build it. He's taken the usual short-cuts.'

'What usual short-cuts?' I ask.

'There, there and there.' Tsunami points. 'The foundations aren't deep enough – that would represent a hundred grand to a building inspector – and the concrete contains too much sand. A lot of the ties that bind – that is, the reinforcing – are missing. Von Franck would argue that the requirements are too severe.' She shrugs. 'Which they are, of course – this crapheap will be standing long after we're gone. But it's still got all the integrity of a toy tower built by a kid. *Clever boy!* Mummy says. *And what else did Miss Phipps teach you today?*' Tsunami shakes her head. 'I call it *kinder-construction* – worth a gold star until the family dog brushes up against it and it topples over.'

'And will it?'

Tsunami shakes her head. 'There'll be leaks and cracks and the paint will peel off but it's safe, so, no, it won't fall down.'

I squint around. The usual nice-suited denizens going about their business. Plus the not-so-neat joker coming out of the building site – the giant nodding to him like he's a friend – smiling.

'Well, if it isn't the private detective,' says the pilgarlic. 'The one obsessed with von Franck!' He doesn't notice Tsunami. 'And now you're on his doorstep. Does that mean you've got something on him?'

'No,' I reply. 'Have you?'

The pilgarlic laughs and he's still laughing as he goes on his way.

'Who was that?'

'A journo called John Curtis, who's proving very helpful because he knows the main players in this case as well as a lot about the industry and he's prepared to share it. I want you to lead the questioning.'

'Why?'

'Because you said you wanted to help.'

The pink phone rings. I check the window. It's Skinny Minnie. 'Hello?'

'Oh, Mr Peel, it's –'

Phones are like guilt in a court of law, a jailable fact until someone proves otherwise.

'What can I do you for?'

'I need more nappies for Fiona, she's run out.'

'Do you want me to see if they'll throw in some baby powder and pins?'

'No, just nappies. Meanwhile, how are you getting on with –?'

I cut across her. 'Yeah, it is nice weather.' I click off and repocket the *Telefunken*. 'She wants nappies,' I tell Tsunami.

'What kind?'

'Just nappies.' I pause before adding, 'For a baby.'

'But does she want them for a crawler, an infant or a toddler? And would they be night-time ones with plastic on the outside or day-time ones without; compact or comfortable; high-capacity or fine-line; medium, large or small; girl or unisex; washable or disposable …?'

I shrug. 'She just said nappies. And she's okay for powder and pins.'

He's the same giant Rube and I came across on our walk-and-talk and we get past him by the simple expedient of me pressing the relevant nerve in his neck while he's distracted by Tsunami tying up a non-existent shoelace. After which we head down the steep track towards a white-painted structure in a corner of the building site. I put on a helmet and yellow vest from a pile near the steps to keep it quasi-legal and Tsunami follows suit. At the other end of the walkway is a door with a *KEEP OUT* sign on it. We go in.

He's seated behind a desk flipping a coin in front of a calendar featuring a heavily underdressed dame hugging a tall building. He doesn't look up as we enter – just goes on flipping the coin: *flip, spin, catch, flip, spin, catch and flip again.*

'This is all I had when I came to this country,' he says. 'Just this one coin and I've still got it: a Romanian *ban* with 1952 – that's the year of my birth – on one side and sheaves of wheat and the sun rising between mountains on the other. It's a symbol of my success, Mr Brown, what's yours?'

By using my current pseudonym, he's thrown me, but that's what he wants to do – a rough-cast man with a face carved out of granite who knows the name I gave the pilgarlic. *Flip, spin, catch, flip, spin, catch and flip again.*

'Success only comes at others' expense,' I tell him. 'Meanwhile, I don't do symbols.'

Tsunami steps forward with a wiggle in her catwalk. 'Look, we haven't got time to frig around, von Franck,' she says.

When he looks up, the hard eyes don't soften.

'That's fine because I don't either. What do you want?'

He doesn't ask how we got in because he's worked it out; he doesn't ask why we're here because the pilgarlic's already told him; and he's leering at Tsunami, who consequently colours and loses her place in the directory. I step forward.

'I want your thugs to stop harassing Madam Blavatsky.'

'Who?'

It figures – it's a big business: Madam B's no more than a small Rorschach blot on a very big bit of paper. I switch to the main drag.

'Where were you on the night of …'

I tell him the night Cock Robin copped it and when von Franck smiles it's like rock splitting.

'Let me guess – that's the night that uppity little unionist was killed, right? And you're on the case because the cops have other fish to fry, am I right? Well, it wasn't me.'

Harry's right: von Franck's personable – for a rock. I shrug. 'That's an answer but it's an answer to another question. What I asked was –'

'I know what you asked but not who you are or who sent you. You're a thug in a red coat in the company of a dame on her way to a fancy-dress ball, accusing me of committing a common-and-garden murder and you expect an answer?'

'Why not, if there's nothing to hide?'

He stops flipping, wraps the coin in his stone fist and when he looks up it's like I'm being measured for a coffin: hard eyes in a hard face, the kind of eyes used to being obeyed, and not far behind them a clever mind doing cartwheels. He shrugs his couldn't-give-a-damn shoulders.

'I knew some idiot might ask so I checked my movements. But after I tell you where I was, you're going to leave and you'll take your girlfriend here with you. That a deal?'

I nod.

'All right,' he says. 'I was walking my dog.'

'Where were you walking your dog?'

'Where I always walk him, in Waverley Cemetery.'

'Any witnesses?'

'Only dead ones.'

'Not much of an alibi, is it?'

'It's enough for a man as rich as I am who no-one's charging.'

He starts flipping the coin again – *flip, spin, catch, flip, spin, catch and flip again* – and he's still flipping as we leave.

Chapter 26

THE DAME ORDERS RISOTTO

The next morning finds Harry's collar crooked and his hair in urgent need of a Hoover. The tables are full of yesterday's plates and silence takes over as someone switches off a lawnmower.

'You got that list I asked for, Harry? The one containing the names of jokers that might have hated Cock Robin? I also need food-handling gloves, if you possess such a thing, as well as a five-pound hammer.'

'Why would I have a five-pound hammer?'

'You've got scales, haven't you? You mightn't have decent coffee or a milkshake machine but you've got to have scales.' Harry nods a reluctant *Yeah*. 'Okay, so I want something that weighs the same as a small dog.'

I slip the list that Harry palms me into the lining of my hat, just below where Tsunami's knife went through it, then do my bit to help by taking the elastic bands off the blatts. The *Terrorgraph*'s front page says:

The city that Jerry built – 9 out of 10 Sydney buildings shonky: Royal Commission into construction industry

Exposé by John Curtis

Accompanying the headlines are photographs of new buildings with cracks in them. Unnamed builders pay unknown politicians big potatoes to get zonings changed. Councils accept bribes to overlook deficiencies. Labour providers threaten disruption if builders don't use their workers. Building materials are stolen and replaced with rubbish …

'Hi!'

I only recognise her because I'm trained to see past the obvious. And the obvious is that Tsunami's exchanged the cat-suit for a nice little number in bloodbath-red with a key hanging off a Magiclip attached to the frock. Even her hair looks good and there's enough black on her eyelashes to induce muscle fatigue in her *orbicular palpebrae*. Behind her stands what I thought was a motor mower – a dinky little 125cc Honda step-over motorbike, a set of crash-hats growing out of the side like carbuncles. I lower the paper.

'You must be somebody's beautiful sister.'

She grunts like she's heard it all before.

'So where are the flowers?'

Harry's ogling from behind his steam-smeared window and I got no riposte worthy of the name.

'What flowers?' I ask.

'When a girl's invited to breakfast on a romantic autumn morning, naturally she expects flowers.'

Harry rushes out and props a menu in front of Tsunami before bending to scrape a dog turd off the footpath. He's done his hair in a comb-over.

'Thank you, darling,' Tsunami murmurs to him, fluttering her mascara, and Harry's dribbling as he leaves; she turns back to me. 'You'll be pleased to know that I solved the nappy problem by buying all twenty-seven varieties. However Fiona needs clothes so we have to go to Minnie's for them.'

I don't know what to say, so I don't say it.

'Cat got your tongue?' Tsunami picks up the menu. 'I hope this dump's better than it looks.'

With the clouds scudding across an azure sky and the leaves on the street trees turning orangey-yellow before fluttering to the footpath, it's a romantic day. But that's not what we're here for. I take a deep breath. 'Look, Tsunami, we've got to —'

'I'll have the risotto.'

I've put the list that Harry produced, along with the two sets of sandwich gloves, in the inside pocket of the orange coat next to the gat; I've got a five-pound window-weight under one arm; and I'm wearing one of the powder-green helmets so as not to attract attention. That's not the case with Tsunami, who's hitched her skirt high enough to cause a pile-up, and if I had any say in the matter I wouldn't be in Bathurst Street on the back of a motor scooter with just enough *oomph* in it to power a ladies' shaver.

'Where am I taking you?' Tsunami yells back to me.

'To see Hunk Waller.'

The first name on the list.

'Who's Hunk Waller?'

'An ex-labourer.'

'Where do we find him?'

'In the Woolloomooloo Refuge for Rogues and Vagabonds.'

I'm shouting to be heard but also because I'm nervous and it's not just due to the dame's driving. The refuge is the soup kitchen where Annie – my ex-squeeze – does voluntary work and I'm going there in company with a dame who, if she looked any sexier, could be arrested for it. Annie dumped me out of hatred but tell that to her subconscious.

'What are you doing here?' Annie's lugging a bucket of soup and, when she sees Tsunami, looks like she wants to throw it at her. 'And who's the tart?'

'Come on, Annie, I can explain …'

'I'm sure you can.' Annie's lips go thinner than a three-legged greyhound's chances in an open sprint as she turns her back on me. 'Only I won't be listening while you're explaining.'

'I need to see someone about a case.'

'With you, Rainbow,' she says over her shoulder, 'everything's a case. And if it wasn't, you'd make it one.' She nods at Tsunami. 'Just like you made her.'

'It's not like it looks.'

'Nothing's ever like it looks,' she says. 'But whether it's like it looks or looks like it isn't, it doesn't change what it is.' She relents; I don't like it when they relent; it's a down payment on misery. 'Who do you want to see – in company with your case?'

'Waller.'

'You mean Hunk?' Annie nods towards an

emaciated-looking joker sucking a straw. 'Hunk's jobless, broke and friendless, so go easy on him, or you'll make him cry and you and your case will have to leave.'

She moves among the tables while I approach the man of straw.

'You Hunk Waller?'

When the skinny man raises his head, he's drooling – much like Harry did over Tsunami – and the bags under his eyes could double as button mushrooms. 'Are you from Jobs-R-Us? Does that mean you got a job for me?'

I tell him no to both questions and he goes back to looking dejected.

'Why are you here then? You look like a gangster and his moll, so go ahead, kill me – you'd be doing the world a favour.'

Chapter 27

IN POTEMKIN'S CLOSE

'I'm not here to kill you, Waller, just to ask you a few questions.' I show him a fistful of fivers. 'You get a couple of these now and the second lot if I like your answers.'

A crafty look appears in his eyes. 'What sort of answers?'

'That's not how it works, Waller – I want fact, not fiction.' I palm him a couple of notes followed by the first question. 'What do you know about Robin Fahey?'

'Robin Who?'

'Robin Fahey – also known as Red Robin, AKA Cock Robin.'

Waller shrugs. 'I know he's dead.'

'How do you know that?'

'There was a celebration at the *Put The Boot Inn*.'

'What were you celebrating?'

'His death, of course. Cock Robin was a bastard. Among other scams he ran an employment agency called Work-R-Us.' Waller sucks at his soup. 'But he only ever found work for people who paid him – never mind any skills they didn't have – and I've never bribed anyone so I stayed jobless. Employers went through Cock Robin or they lost building contracts and workers had to go through him or they didn't get work.' Waller shrugs. 'I tried to get a job without using him and ended up getting bashed.'

'Did you kill him?'

He looks at the money. 'Is that a question or an accusation?'

'A question.'

'Do I get the extra dix if I say yeah?'

'That's not the way it works, Waller. I don't want the right answer, I want the truth.'

His eyes hang off the money. 'All right, nah, I didn't kill him.'

'Do you know who did?'

He nods. 'Yeah.'

'Who?'

'Someone that hated him and also had the guts to do it.'

'Why might anyone hate Cock Robin?'

'Does my answer get me another tenner?'

'No.'

Waller grimaces. 'He was a bully. For instance, everyone knew he bashed his missus.' He gets the thought long after everyone else got it. 'Hey, she probably done it!'

'Got any other names – apart from the wife?'

Waller gives me a few more names and most of them tally with those on Harry's list but I give the down-and-out the second dix anyway and make like I'm leaving before pretending to remember I forgot something and hand him the window sash. 'Hold this for a moment for me, would you, Hunk?'

He goes to take the weight but drops it. He tries to pick it up but can't. It wasn't him.

The shots go wide. I like it when shots go wide. They're big ones, the kind that come out of a Taurus Raging Bull Magnum or a Colt Python. We're scootering down Liverpool when the first slug whistles by, I yank the dame off the bike with the hand that's not holding the window weight and the bike does a cartwheel and smacks into a wall. I give Tsunami the twice-over and by the time I get around to the gunman, he's gone. I can't see Tsunami's face because of the visor but I can tell she's not happy.

'Are you hurt?' I ask her.

She struggles to her feet, tugging her torn skirt over her thighs as she rips off her helmet. I can see her face. I was right, she's not happy.

'You don't know the half of it.' She checks the bike: the fairing's cracked but the front wheel's still straight and when she presses the starter, the thing still goes. 'Know what? Being with you is like being in a war zone. You owe me a dress.'

We're in George Street outside the Queen Victoria Building, opposite the Hilton. A couple of years back someone planted a bomb here and now someone's shooting out of the hotel. Going by where the slugs landed, the angle of fire was 30 degrees off horizontal. I check the relevant windows but see nothing but pigeons. I turn back to the dame. She's still not happy.

'Anyone hate you enough to take a potshot at you, Tsunami?'

'I'm just a girl, soldier. Otherwise I'm an engineer in the building industry – which means no-one likes me.'

'Anyone in particular?'

'No,' she says, and I know she's telling the truth because she's still angry. 'Now, you owe me a dress.'

Darkness is falling as the dame swings her leg off the bike and if I hadn't ducked I'd need to make an unscheduled visit to the dentist. The street sign says we're in Potemkins Close but for my money the name wears an apostrophe. I check out the street and discover too many hovels, none of them wired to the free-for-all soporific, Foxtail. I can't see Pandora and, if the gunman's nearby, I can't see him either. Just two stray dogs doing what stray dogs do, a cat, and a yellow Transit van, the writing on the side telling anyone who wants to know that it can be trusted.

'Bugger, hell and damn,' Tsunami mutters.

'What's wrong?'

'I've lost the bloody key, that's what's wrong.'

Chapter 28

THE ANGRY SHADOW

'Come on, it's not the end of the world.'

'But how can we get into the house without a key?'

'We break in.'

The figure in the van isn't a cardboard cut-out which means going in by the front door could be fatal. I take the pencil torch out of my pocket but don't switch it on until we get to the garbage lane. If you don't want to attract attention, always take the garbage lane. In any situation, I'm careful; when jokers start taking potshots, I'm even more careful; and when I'm entering a joint where someone's been murdered, I'm more careful still. I stuff the butt-end of the torch in my mouth, get myself in the workshed, and recheck the shadow board.

After that I take the torch out of my gob and head up Minnie's garden path, one hand gripping the weight and my arms out and slightly forward like James Cagney in every movie he ever died in, while the dame's my angry shadow. Still the same cop-ploughed ground; still the weeds; and still the bench where Skinny Minnie sat feeding Fiona. I tuck the weight under my arm, palm Tsunami a pair of sandwich gloves, jam the torch back in my cakehole, put on my gloves, do the necessary with the fuses, and picklock the door.

'Why all this cloak-and-dagger stuff?' she asks.

I remove the torch and heft the weight. 'Because I'm a cloak-and-dagger kind of guy. Also I want to stay alive. We've come for baby things but, going by the van parked outside, we could end up with a lot more than we came for.'

The scent of the flowers the cop brought Skinny Minnie hits me like a smack in the kisser as we enter the loungeroom. Dust, mould, the stench of flower-pot soil and the scent of flowers. No-one's disturbed the length of cotton I taped across the hallway when I last visited. Which doesn't mean nobody's been here.

There's no such thing as luck – luck's for lickspittles. Outside of comic books, Superman's not flying to the rescue if I make a mistake. Trust to luck and you might as well sit on a plastic duck, sucking your thumb on a merry-go-round in a fun fair. Cock Robin's been murdered, Pandora's after me, a thwarted cop's keen to make an arrest, I've been used as a punching bag, a gunman's taken a potshot at us, and a Foxtail van's parked in a street where no-one's got Foxtail …

'Wouldn't it make our lives a lot easier if we turned on the lights?' Tsunami asks.

'If we turn on the lights, there's a good chance we'll no longer *have* lives. A van's out there with someone at the controls and the writing on the side says it shouldn't be. The driver doesn't live next door because: a) the equipment in a Foxtail van is too expensive to leave in the street and b) the van wouldn't be parked outside Minnie's if the driver lived next door.'

'But who'd stake out an innocent little townhouse?'

'First of all, this joint ain't all that innocent. And second, the driver could be one of too many people with both the motive and the resources to do a stake-out. So ask yourself who –'

'It's the cop who's trying to crack onto Minnie, isn't it?' she says. 'The reason why Minnie's at my place instead of here.'

The scent of flowers is a reminder of the strength of the cop's motivation as the front door crashes open, followed by the click of a light switch that doesn't work, followed by the click of a torch that does. Boots crunch up the hall.

'Wh – what do we do now?' she whispers.

I chuck her the penlight. 'Hang onto that and keep it turned on – it'll tell me where you are.'

'But it'll tell *him* where I am, too.'

I drag the window weight out from under my arm. 'Yeah, that, too.'

There's acting in self-defence and there's stupidity and hitting a cop with a five-pound length of cast iron is stupidity except when you've got no choice. As Richardson hammers up the hallway, the beam of his torch illuminates the dame. It's enough to distract him and I get him in the ribs but the weight's no good for closer combat so I chuck it, Tsunami screams and the pencil torch flies through the air and lands at my feet, while the cop goes for his Glock. I dive.

I got three advantages:

I'm bigger than he is;

I may have fractured his rib; and

He's distracted by Tsunami.

But fights don't always go with the advantage. Richardson's got his gun out and he's holding it near my ear – which makes this a matter of lithe or deaf. I roll away, see a flash by my left eye and hear a deafening report as he fires. On the roll, I remember Richardson held out his *right* hand when he asked for my ID, keeping his *left* hand free in case he needed to go for his gat. So I go for his *left* arm – his gun arm – and my grappling fingers find a wrist, followed by the gat. I try to get a grip on it, remembering too late that cops put *carbonitride* on their weaponry to counter corrosion, which makes them slippery. Also I'm wearing condom gloves. Richardson gets his arm free and the second slug plays follow-the-leader with the first …

Chapter 29

POTSHOT

In the eternal battle of good versus evil there's no smart money on who'll win. There's fear but no favour and the results are random. I've got my hands on the gun but the cop's out to do damage, the sounds emerging from his throat the sort of noise you'd expect from a predator – a bestial shriek, a bellow from a cave, a roar as the creature sinks its fangs into the neck of its victim. I tear myself free only to find myself on roller-skates. A whiteside finds the pencil torch and I go down, my head hitting the floor and momentarily putting me out to it. But a moment's all he needs. I'm flat on my back and when I open my eyes, he's standing, legs apart and knees bent in the firing position, arms straight out in front of him, hands knuckle-white on the gat, torso forward to deal the death blow, face uplit by the torch, which shadows his eyes and mouth, turning his face into a skull.

A .45 GAP slug's only short but when fired at close range from a police-issue Glock it leaves no room for manoeuvre. At a distance, cops go for maximum body mass. But I'm not at a distance so he's aiming for my eyes and I'm staring down the barrel as his forefinger squeezes the lock-lever before going for the trigger. Even before they hit I can feel them — the bullets, the *blue beans* — as the gun's mechanism reaches tipping point. I close my eyes to death: *Imogene,* I hear myself murmur, *Aunt Rube, my dear little dead sister, Dad, Mum, Annie …*

Followed by a crash, a scream, then terrible silence.

The cop's gun hand is empty and his eyes are emptier still but somehow I'm still alive. I roll the dead weight off me, find the little torch and jam it in my mouth. The flowerpot Tsunami chucked shattered when it hit him. I work my hands over his body to find a lot of dirt, the remains of the pot and wetness. An artery is pumping Richardson's lifeblood out of him and signing my death warrant. You don't kill a cop in this city and get away with it. After this, I'll be lucky to be mining opals in Coober Pedy. The light comes on; I spit out the torch.

'There are some things upstairs called Magiclips,' I tell Tsunami. 'They'll connect anything to anything and you'll find them with the kid's things.'

I fight to recall the relevant section of *Gray's Anatomy: the sheath of the artery should be divided to a sufficient extent to allow for the introduction of the ligature, but no further …* I find the severed ends of the artery, press them together and the blood slows. Behind me, I hear Tsunami. She hands me the clips. I transfer the two ends of the severed artery into one hand and seal the ends off with the Magiclips.

'Did I kill him?' Tsunami asks.

I feel his pulse. It's as lively as a dead rat. 'Not yet.'

Richardson's eyes are fluttering, his arms spread out like he's offering absolution – or begging for it.

I jerk my head at the phone. 'Dial 000, Tsunami, and dial it fast.' I hear her pad down the hall, pick up the handset, tap out the numbers and rap out the necessary details, before hanging up and returning.

'Now get the nappies,' I tell her.

It takes a lot of nappies to stanch the bloodflow but there are still some left after I manage it. Only then do I sit back.

'We got to get out of here.'

When I turn up at Harry's next morning, the play bike's already outside, the dame's already seated and Harry's already hovering. She's wearing a little silk number that barely covers her shoulders, there are dark smudges under her eyes that didn't come out of a beauty case and she comes straight to the point.

'I had to throw the flowerpot, Brownie.'

'It's all right.'

'I didn't know it would kill him.'

'He's not dead yet.'

'I'm sick of being a babysitter.'

'I didn't ask for your help.'

'I don't mean looking after *you*, I mean Philomena, or whatever her name is.'

'Look, I'm more than happy to go it alone from here,' I say. 'You came in handy last night, chucking that pot, but ...'

'Richardson was just another enemy and it was

just like throwing another hand grenade.'

'… but you could get yourself killed. Apart from which,' I add hopefully, 'you must have a lot of work to do.'

'So I'll put in an appearance at the office. But I finish what I start,' she adds and the sun ricochets off her bare shoulders like shot silk.

She pauses while Harry serves the coffee – a nice, clean little cup with a heart carefully worked into the froth for Tsunami; a dirty, cracked mug with slops in the saucer for me. I take a slug of the muck and shove it aside. I like coffee but this ain't coffee.

'That's not how I run a case. Solving a murder isn't some kind of social outing. The cops have let someone off but are now busy framing someone else. Which means that somewhere out there is a killer.'

Tsunami looks downcast. It must be the coffee.

'But surely I can help.'

Like I say, waves change. Tsunami's like an idle surf licking at a sandbank – frothy driblets caressing the shore while the big thumper's building up its killer load far out to sea. I pick up the *Terrorgraph* to give me time to think, only it doesn't do anything of the sort. Because the front page – as well as several more pages inside – feature a stoush between von Franck and the politician known as Clean Fill, the main entry reading:

A Fill and Franck Exchange?

Chapter 30

IF YOU PRICK US ...

A billboard reading *BLUEBEARD* – make that *BLUE*BIRD – fills the background while the two combatants are down and dirty, a lot of onlookers trying to pull them apart. One picture shows Clean Fill attempting to run, with von Franck in pursuit. Another shot shows them slugging it out to a backdrop of a passing bus with *WELCOME TO SYDNEY* on its side.

It takes a lot to keep people happy in this burg but this story should help: a billionaire and a politician down in the gutter with the rest of the *Terrorgraph* readers – proof positive that jokers at the pointy end of our plutocracy are no different from the rest of us. The big type says: *WE PAID A QUARTER OF A MILLION DOLLARS FOR THESE PHOTOS AND THIS IS THE REASON WHY ...* Followed by a lot of frothing-at-the-mouth articles – with only one in exculpation:

A FRIENDLY STOUSH

A Pair of Not-So-Ordinary Men Reveal their Human Side

JOHN CURTIS reports:

They've been mates since attending school together. As friends they've had their ups and downs but who hasn't?

There's the mandatory journey down memory lane before the piece winds up with:

Just another blue

The two blokes in this stoush — the cabinet minister and the developer — might be tall poppies. But in the end they're just like the rest of us — a couple of knockabout guys giving vent to their feelings, simply because they have feelings.

They might be down today but they'll bounce back tomorrow, role models for the rest of us. Take the word of one who knows: this bit of biffo is news simply because of who these men are — a pair of Aussie success stories. And in the end, all it proves is that they're human. As the Bard said: 'If you prick us, do we not bleed?'

I look up. Tsunami's eyes are on me. She shrugs. 'I saw it on the late night news while trying to get Fiona to sleep. Von Franck's our man all right, while the rest of those names on your list are no more than Caution's bedfellows. I knew it when we confronted him and I feel it again now. Just look at that face.'

The face in the photo's contorted with rage. But a face doesn't determine guilt. If von Franck killed Cock Robin, what was the motive? Would a successful man risk a lifetime's work in a moment? And if he was angry with his old schoolmate, what could have been –

Tsunami gives voice to my thoughts. 'What could have upset von Franck enough for him to …? It must have been something that this mate of his – what's his name …?'

'Clean Fill.'

'… said.' Tsunami shrugs. 'But people *say* things …'

I find myself thinking aloud.

'What about the photographer? What was he doing there? Good photographers don't grow on trees, Tsunami, and this was a good one – a quarter-of-a-million smackeroos good, going by what the *Terrorgraph* paid. The question is: how come this good photographer was in the right place at the right time?'

Harry returns. Harry does that – he returns, like bad food. I note the photo credit: Peter Parkinson.

'Want anything more?' Harry asks, looking hopefully at Tsunami.

I follow his gaze. Tsunami's an amoeba – seeming to change shape, attitude and sexual orientation as quickly as a rabbit. I stand.

'See you around, Tidal Wave,' I say. 'I got a couple of jobs to do and – like you said – you got to go to the orifice. I'll give you a bell in a week or so.'

'Why not sooner?'

'That's not the way it works.'

Because the way it works is that I go back to the *Wooden No* and get the toolbag. After that I don a pair of grey workingman's overalls from Vinnie's, pick up a yellow Port-a-rail from a building site and hoof it to Bondi, where I locate the relevant phone hydrant, set up my little fence and, using the tools from the boat, remove the cover. I flick through the connections until I come to von Franck's, attach the buzz-cock then replace the cover. And after that, I pay a visit to the photographer.

Parkinson's office is in The Rocks, a hole in the wall at the top of a set of stairs next to a souvenir shop flogging genuine artefacts made overseas. I pull the fedora well down over my eyes and Parkinson doesn't look up as I shove open the mottled-glass door with *DONT ENTER* written on it and enter. A window produces just enough light to reveal a top-of-the-lion digital camera with a snout on it like an elephant's bo-diddly. It's sitting on a desk that contains one too many knotholes, together with a notepad, pencil and phone.

'Can't you read?'

I shrug. 'Why waste time reading when I can look at all the dirty pictures? Are you Parkinson – as in the disease?'

He's big and of a certain age and uncertain temperament and when he finally looks up he's not smiling. 'That's my line, mate. Yeah, I'm him – what's your excuse?'

'I'm a private investigator.'

'I can see how that could be a problem.' He tilts back his chair and considers me over his gut. 'What have you got for me, Mr Gumshoe? A nice little old-fashioned slab of adultery? An insurance scammer hefting pianos? A peasant poking a princess?'

I feel dirty just being here, like the air's foetid and crawling with maggots. I square my shoulders and come to the point. 'How did you get ringside tickets to the von Franck–Clean Fill bout?'

The paparazzo's face gets a stonewall look to it and filters come down over his piggy eyes. 'Who wants to know?'

'Like I said I'm a –'

'Yeah, I know what you *said* you were – what I haven't heard yet is *who*.' He reaches for his camera, the one with the long-range snout on it. 'More important, who you're working for.'

He's picked up the camera and he's got it up to one piggy eye with his finger on the danger button when I reach across and snap it out of his hands before he's got a chance to snap me.

'You'll get it back when you tell me why you were there.'

'That's theft!'

'So is taking people's pictures when they don't want you to. Who told you there'd be a fight?'

Chapter 31

... DO WE NOT BLEED?

Parkinson's sitting and I'm standing and I've got a firm grip on his livelihood. My hat's well down over my eyes so the eye-spy positioned at 11 o'clock in the ceiling can't see my face and I'm capable of anything. Who knows with private defectives?

'All right,' he mutters. 'I got a tip-off.'

'Who from?'

His eyes go even craftier than they were before and he goes coyer than a virgin in a harem. 'A little bird told me.'

'Heard of the Marquis of Queensberry Rules? That's when you get three-minute rounds, there's no hitting below the belt and if you stay down long enough they call it a knockout. Well, that's them and this is me: I know no rules – apart from the facts. And the facts are that if you don't give me a name on the count of three you lose your Box Brownie and a lot more besides. One –'

His eyes shift to the door but it's an old trick so my eyes don't shift with his. Instead I bring the camera over my head like I'm about to throw it.

'Two –'

When he drags his eyes away from the door, there's a scared look in them.

'All right, I'll talk.'

'Of course you will. And it'll be the truth, too, because otherwise your expensive little camera goes out the window.'

So he tells me, only what he tells me *isn't* the truth. And I know it's not the truth because his eyes go walkabout to the door once more as he slings me a story about von Franck being a playboy who playboyed Clean Fill's wife and when Clean Fill's daughter found out about it she told her father who got angry with von Franck and – he winds up, like I'm still wet behind the ears – the rest is history …

'*His*-tory or *your* story, Parkinson? Because what you left out is what I want to know. Namely *how* you knew the fight was on. You've got one last chance: *Who told you?*'

But Parkinson doesn't reply because he can't. There's an old saying that the only good *paparazzo* is a dead *paparazzo* which is what Parkinson's just become – a third eye appearing in the centre of his forehead about the size and shape of a .45 slug. I pirouette and drop, my gat transferring itself from the under-shoulder holster to my fist as another bullet wings over my head and a figure I only see the tail-end of disappears out of the *DONT ENTER* doorway.

I close the two of the dead man's eyes I can do anything about, remove the tape from the closed-circuit television camera, gouge the photo device out of the extra knothole in the desk, tear the top sheet off the pad by the phone, and flip the sign on the doorknob so it reads *DO NOT DISTRUB* as I make my departure.

In these days of hi-tech surveillance, people forget the imprint of a telephone message remains on the undersheet of a writing pad after the top page is removed, and that's what I subject to the necessary treatment on board the *Wooden No.* And what I come up with mightn't be much – no more than a four-letter word – but it's enough to give me a lot to think about as I row back to shore and take a bus into the city.

BLUE, the word says. But is that *blue* as in *stoush*? Or *blue* as in *mistake. Blue* as in *sad* maybe … What about *blue* as in *Once in a blue moon.* Or *blue blood* or *university blue* or *blue movie* or *true blue* – the last being a reference to butchers' aprons which, because of their colour, somehow manage to hide bloodstains … *Blue beans* are bullets, a *blue fish* is a shark. What about the flag that departing ships display – the *Blue Peter*? Or *blue ruin*, as in gin; *blue talk*, as in indecent language; or …

Blue is as *blue* does and in the end all I'm left with is the fact that *BLUE* means both too much and too little and I put it to one side and get on with what I've got – which is little more than a fine day and a listening device attached to a phone hydrant.

I set up shop at a bus stop where I pretend my big white earphones are playing Beethoven's *Fifth*, the first four notes of which represent Fate. *Dah-dah-te-daaah* … I wave my arms around, conducting as I hum – it keeps the flies away. *Dah-dah-te-dah* … A couple of surfers give me a wide berth and an old dame smiles uncertainly as she hobbles past. *Dah-te-dah-dah; dah-dah-te-dah* …

But all I'm really hearing is the kind of noise allegedly made by rice bubbles – a *snap, crackle, poopedy-scoop* – until a voice comes out of the stratosphere, saying:

'*That you, Elephant?*'

'*Who else would it be?*'

'*Pesto wants more.*'

'*Pesto always wants more.*'

'*That's why they call him Pesto – you know, as in pest?*'

General laughter. Von Franck – he must be *Elephant* – gives the relevant instructions and there's a click followed by silence. Paranoids reckon intelligence agencies bug everyone but we're assured by those same agencies that they only collect *metadata* – who rang whom and when – and then only when those calls involve people the spooks believe are menaces to society. In which case, von Franck's in the clear because he's clearly too rich to be a menace to anyone. *Dah-dah-te-dah-te-dah-dah* … Another call:

'*Hey, Maestro!*'

'*Dithyramb!*'

'*Guess what? The Premier's come good – we got the okay for the western subdivision.*'

'How much did that cost?'
'Nowhere near what it'll earn.'

More general laughter. Von Franck and his mob are a merry little gang of toadstools but they've got a lot to laugh about – the happiness that comes with making a lot of money for themselves and misery for everyone else. More of the same, a morning – make that *mourning* – of more of the same. But I'm not here to hear about corruption, I'm here for –

'Mr von Franck?'

The voice is respectful, verging on sycophancy.

'Who's this?'

'This is the Minister for Development's secretary, Mr von Franck. The Minister says he'd be delighted to accept your kind invitation for a cruise aboard The Holy Profit *to show quote there's no ill feeling over our little contretemps the other day unquote. Is there anything he should bring?'*

'No, only something he shouldn't – his conscience.'

General laughter. After which:

Secretary: *'I'm sorry but could I have that date again?'*

'Why do your own barking when you own a dog? Here's my personal assistant.'

The PA comes on; she's got a sweet voice, honey mixed with an overdose of strychnine, and *Yes*, she says, *the cruise is next Thursday – 7 pm to midnight –* and I commit the date and time to memory.

After which I doff the earphones, unhitch the bug and call Tsunami.

Chapter 32

FIGURES IN A LANDSCAPE

The tide comes in and goes out again. Annie still doesn't want to know me and neither does Rory; Salina still won't let me see Imogene; and Ruby's still crook. 'Forget about me, Rainbow,' she said the last time I called. 'Bury yourself in your work …'

Rube's right, so I keep on with the early-morning exercise regime; do the ballet exercises and the laps at Bondi; overdose on Harry's coffee; watch the high-rise buildings rear ever higher on Sydney's skyline; patch the boat until it becomes patches on patches; and watch the to-and-fro of *The Holy Profit* – von Franck's cruiser, a modest little vessel roughly the size of the *Titanic*.

The following Thursday night, clouds cover the moon and Tsunami's a black shadow under a streetlamp as she settles her bike on its haunches on the inner flank of Bondi's Campbell Parade. I quarter the area – the sparkle of the main drag, the cold stretch of the promenade, the black sea – but apart from the gentle flip-flop of the surf on the night sand and the murmur of lovers on the swings, there's nothing but the sound of Tsunami sniffling as she draws near, and the strong stench of camphor.

'You can still change your mind,' I say.

'Why?' She hauls out a baby-wipe to stifle a sneeze as she glances at the lovers before bringing her eyes back to me. 'After tending to a sick kid all week, this is a walk in the proverbial.'

'All right, there's a good chance we're going to meet up with dogs and/or armed guards and you're reeking of a highly aromatic sinus-clearer because you happen to have a cold. They'll know without looking that they've got company. Which means you've either got to take a rain check on this outing or ditch the medication.'

Once we're sorted, I go over the plan. We're here for a reason, which is to link von Franck to the killing of Cock Robin – or not, as the case may be. The murder mightn't have been committed by von Franck in person – like he said: *If you've got a dog, why do your own barking?* But he's smart enough to know that the more dogs he uses the more there'll be to bite him.

Bondi used to be the kind of suburb where punters slipped out of their trackies, kicked back on the sand and relaxed. But that was before von Franck and his mob built hotels for *über*-rich tourists and the toffee-nosed coffee houses followed. Now all you got to do is pay and the garb's Givenchy.

Von Franck's place leans so far over the beach that

it looks like a potential suicide. I've supplemented
the misinformation from *Home Incredible* with the
plans that Blueprint Eddie (add *blueprint* to the
list of things blue) filched from Council. Which
reveal that, in addition to the six bedrooms, there's
a 32-seat movie theatre, a games room, a sauna and
a heated indoor pool that Samantha Ricecake would
feel at home in – plus a guardhouse in a bunker
under the billiard room.

The tide's in and the waves are licking at my rubber
duckies as I stuff my hat in my backpack, don the
balaclava and abseil up the cliff with Tsunami
behind me. It's a long way up, Tsunami's coughing
by the time we get there, and her coughing's
attracting attention – as I coil up the rope ready for
a quick departure, somewhere in the house a dog
starts barking.

Our presence has also activated the sensor lights. I
park Tsunami by the lights, put on the night-vision
glasses, move to a window that's well within range of
the cameras, tape a fist-sized section of glass next to
the window lock, do the cut, remove the glass, then
lead Tsunami around to the front door. She clears
her throat.

'I thought you didn't do front doors,' she says.

'I still don't,' I reply. 'But the guards will be
attracted to the window and when they are' – I
waggle my gat: a Chinese-made BBQ-901 general-
anaesthetic gun – 'I feed them the sleep juice.'

'Are we looking for anything in particular?'

I keep my eye on the hole in the window. 'A pair of kingsize plimsolls complete with garden mud from Minnie's on their soles would be nice.' I hear two sets of footsteps – one heavy, the other light. 'Failing that, whatever's on offer. But first we got to neutralise the guards.'

The moon's on holiday but I'm wearing the head-mounted Gen-3 ATN PS15-21 night-vision binoculars and they pick up the guards as they round the corner to the tune of the dog barking inside the house, two figures showing up in my Gen-3 lenses coloured blue.

Not possible, I tell myself. But anything's possible, even the appearance of the pair of goons that thumped me outside Clean Fill's, who would also fit Mismatch's description of the thugs that broke her arm – one big, the other small. Both are wearing the same kind of head-mounted Gen-3 binoculars I'm wearing, the tall one's got a gun and the little one's wielding a cricket bat – but at a guess, I'd say he's not looking for a nice little game of elevenses.

That's when Tsunami sneezes and that's when the tall one's head flicks our way.

'There he is!' High voice. 'The window was a trick – pincer him!'

'What do we do now?' Tsunami asks.

'We keep our balaclavas on.'

As directed by the tall man, the small man – *Lofty*, Piano Girl said he was called – stays where he is, while the tall, skinny one – by the same logic, he's probably *Chubby* – goes around the side. I could anaesthetise the bat-wielder after which me and

Tsunami could escape down the cliff before the tall one reaches us, but I don't like failure – never have. I motion Tsunami with the Barbecue.

'Get out there with your hands up.'

'But he'll shoot me!'

'Not with a cricket bat, he won't.'

'But –'

'Remember your training, soldier!'

'What the –!' cries the little one. After which, he yells, 'Watch out, Fat Lady!'

Chapter 33

DEEP BLUE

Fat Lady? The barking inside the house goes up a couple of notches as the little man hesitates, a tailender at the crease with the light fading who's desperately in need of a six. I shoot him with the anaesthetic gun, he goes down and the bat drops from his hands.

'Gotcha!'

The voice is too close for comfort. I stand my ground.

'Drop the gat!' says the voice belonging to the figure that the small man called Fat Lady.

When Tsunami cracks her over the head with the bat, the Fat Lady goes down like a foot-long sandwich. I check their pulses; they're both as slow as Rory's thought processes. With Lofty anaesthetised and the Fat Lady counting canaries, we've got ten minutes, fifteen tops.

Whatever door the guards came out of, it's closed, so I reach through the hole in the window and flick the latch. There's a growl, followed by a black-and-tan bloodhound and just enough time to unleash the sleep-maker before it gets me.

There's something wrong with this scenario but there isn't time to work it out. I've got enough in my sugar bowl without working things out. The lights in the house are on and there's no need to turn them off because both the guards and the dog are accounted for. But the cameras are still operative so I remind Tsunami to keep her balaclava on while we search the house. Upstairs are the promised en suites, which gives me just under two minutes a room; I hear the dame moving about downstairs as I check walls, floor and furnishings. Nothing, nothing and more nothing.

When we get outside again the dog's just coming to and the salt air's shimmering over a building that didn't feature in the blueprint – a small, blocky structure situated on the northern boundary of the block, its door open. Tsunami looks nervous.

'How long before they wake up?'

I move towards the open door. 'Couple of minutes.'

The headlamp doesn't work when deprived of starlight so I use the pencil torch. There's the usual electric appliances plus the usual workbench with the usual tools on it.

'Ah!' I murmur.

Tsunami squeezes in beside me. 'What have you found?'

I shine the torch on the tools. A faint glimmer shines back.

'What do you see, Tsunami?'

'Just some tools.' She shrugs. 'But von Franck's a builder – you'd expect him to have tools, wouldn't you?'

'But what do you notice about them?'

'That they're rusty because the door's open and the salt air's got to them.'

'Except' – I hold up the wrench that's on top of the pile of tools – 'this one's not rusty.'

'That means that it doesn't belong here, which makes it the murder weapon,' says Tsunami. 'Case solved, end of story.'

'Sorry, but it's only the beginning.'

'Why? Doesn't it mean that von Franck did it? All we have to do now is tell the police where we found the wrench, Richardson will no longer have a hold over Minnie and she can go home.' Tsunami reaches her climax. 'And take her bloody kid with her.'

I heft the wrench. 'While I'm pretty certain this is the murder weapon, I'm equally sure I'm not judge, jury and executioner. And going to the cops won't work because: a) We're somewhere we're not meant to be; b) von Franck's protected by his wealth and; c) I can't go to the cops.'

'Why?'

'Because I don't exist.' I recall Salina's words. 'I'm a non-person – proof of my existence being either non-existent or destroyed. And if I go to the cops I'll exist and that'll be the end of the line.'

'Why?'

'Because I'll be thrown into jail for existing. And after that – after I exist – I'll be at the mercy of everyone I don't want to be at the mercy of – the cops, the taxman, bill collectors, assorted mercenaries, and Pandora.'

'All right, what do we do now?'

'We get the hell out of here before the dog, the Fat Lady, Lofty or all three wake from their sleepy-byes and come after us. And we dump the wrench on the way.'

At least the tide's out as we get ourselves down the cliff and along the rock platform. As we hit the platform, I chuck the wrench out to sea.

The wind rock-and-rolls the *Wooden No* and through the porthole I make out the Harbour, the Bridge, the real estate of the Eastern Suburbs, the Botanic Gardens they're talking about developing, the Opera House which probably ditto and the inevitable flock of cranes dragging the city ever higher into the unknown.

The boat lists and I get myself into the bilge and start doing the bail-out. It's like lightning's split the sea and the deep blue hole under the boat goes on forever.

The phone rings.

'Brownie?'

It's Tsunami.

'Could be,' I say.

'Something's happened.'

'What?'

'It's all over the news. You wouldn't want me to say on the phone.'

'I'll be right over.'

There's a pause as I hear a voice and a baby crying in the background. 'Minnie wants you to get some nappies on the way.'

'Would that be crawlers, infants or toddlers; the night-time ones with plastic on the outside or day-time ones without; compact or comfortable;

medium, large or small; girl or unisex; washable or disposable –?'

'Just nappies – and hurry.'

Chapter 34

ARTERIAL MOTIVE

No paper boy cycles down to the shore with the early-morning newspapers, singing sea shanties as he rows among the boats, chucking rolled-up *Terror-diddlies* down gangways. I like it like that – there's enough trouble in the world without having to read about it. But, forewarned, I buy a newspaper from the inconvenience store where I get the nappies, reading it in the back of the Deluxe Blue hansom cab on the way to Tsunami's.

DETECTIVE DEAD
HERO HACKED
MAGICLIP MURDER
ARTERIAL MOTIVE?

I work my way through the contorted phraseology to find what the paper's saying.

A hero has died, the victim of an apparently motiveless slaying. In the course of his duties, Detective Sergeant Richard Richardson was attending a house that was the scene of a recent murder – only to fall victim to possibly the same mystery slayer himself.
The recipient of a Police Medal for Bravery after an incident on a building site, Sergeant Richardson was

allegedly subjected to kinky sexual practices as he lay supine on the murder house floor. Bullets recovered from the crime scene show that he tried to defend himself, but to no avail.

Responding to an emergency call from an unknown caller, detectives and paramedics discovered the police hero lying in a pool of blood. Portions of a shattered ceramic pot were allegedly found, along with a number of nappies and two pins known as Magiclips.

Detective Richardson was rushed to hospital but died shortly after admittance. Investigating police are looking for …

The cab drops me outside Vegan Nirvana in Balmain and I complete the rest of the journey on foot. When I arrive I palm Minnie the Disposable Girls Reversible Dri-Tots while Tsunami hands me a mug.

'Is that how you like it?'

'If it's coffee I like it.'

She lowers her voice and raises it all at the same time. 'They're trying to pin this latest murder on Minnie as well. It's in all the news and the cops are buzzing around like sex-crazed hornets. They're calling Minnie a *gangster's moll.*'

Sunlight gleams on the French-polished furniture, Skinny Minnie's perched innocently on a daybed feeding Fiona and from somewhere outside come the sweet strains of an étude by Chopin.

'They don't really think it's her,' I say. 'Blaming her

makes it look like they're doing something while at the same time the real killer – that is, of Cock Robin and maybe also the photographer – relaxes and maybe makes a mistake. If that's all they're doing, then Minnie's safe – at least for the moment.'

I speak with an authority I don't feel. If Minnie was in trouble before, she's in double trouble now.

The coffee's better than Harry's – then again, anything's better than Harry's – and if Tsunami's face was any more drawn, she'd be a charcoal sketch by da Vinci.

'So what do we do now?'

I nod at Minnie. 'I'm going to see a journo about a hero.'

'What about me?'

'You've got to stay here and keep an eye on Minnie.'

I find the pilgarlic nursing a beer on the other side of happiness in the bar of the Scribes' Swill in good old downtown Slurry Hills.

'Top cop dies – nursing mother suspected of second slaying,' he says. 'Only the good die young.'

I order a first for me and a fourth, fifth or tenth for Curtis.

'Tell me about Richardson being good.'

'He –' Curtis looks cunning. 'You got something in exchange, Mr Private Defective?'

I hand him the beer. 'Here's a down payment on sorrow,' I say. 'Tell me about your hero.'

While he talks, I figure the scribe for a Pollyanna. Despite the hardboiled act, he only ever sees people's nice side. Von Franck is Mother Teresa, Richardson was the Messiah and Curtis doesn't tell me anything I couldn't have read in the *Terrorgraph* – but then, he probably wrote it.

'Richard Richardson,' he says, 'the recipient of a Police Medal for Bravery after an incident on a building site, met his tragic end at the hands of an assassin bent on …'

It's like listening to a talking typeface but I still hear him out. And after I hear him out, I buy him another lip-loosener and ask the question I really want answered.

'Tell me about the incident.'

'What incident?'

'The one in which Richardson was a hero.'

On the turn, Curtis knocks over the glass with the outline of Australia and *AHA* on the side. Once the letters might have stood for *Australian Hotels Association* but now they just spell *Aha!* The barmaid mops the beer off the bar-top and I order a new one.

'What's your particular interest in all this?'

'I'm not *particularly* interested in anything – except a chat. I'm at a loose end due to the End-of-the-world Financial Crisis and I'm just trying to make ends meet – you know, as in *End, I'd like you to meet End.*' I stand. 'Okay then, I'll get out of your hair.'

Goal number one in journalism – even before the

truth – is to hold onto your contacts. He grabs my elbow.

'You have to understand I – just lost a mate.'

I spread my hands like I'm the Pope or the Daily Llama. 'I didn't realise Richardson was a particular mate.'

Curtis bows his head over his beer. 'Us old-time journos were put through the hoops – that is, we did the rounds. When I was on Police Rounds, Richardson and I hung together. So, do you want to know about the hero?'

'Only if you want to tell me.'

Chapter 35

UNDER COVER OF LIGHT ...

Several years ago, Richard Richardson was just another young constable when he got his big chance.

'It was a time of great unease in the building industry,' Curtis says. 'There'd been the so-called Green Bans, but when they stopped, the unions became irrelevant again – they were rebels without a cause who had lost public sympathy. Then along came a man who was half-crook, half-saviour. Due to his politics, they called him *Robin the Red* or *Red Robin* – but eventually he came to be known as Cock Robin.'

I finish my drink and order several more for both of us.

'As General Secretary of the Building Labourers' Federation, Cock Robin organised a strike on one of von Franck's building sites. But von Franck, being von Franck, fought back and negotiations ended in fisticuffs. Iron bars that were meant for reinforcing – there's irony for you – were produced. It was striking workers versus scabs. Then Richardson rode into the *mêlée …*'

'And won himself a Police Medal for bravery. Is that when he turned crooked? You know, *Under cover of light, darkness reigned?* And that union trouble – did Richardson foment it?'

'Ferment?'

'*Fo*-ment – as in *heat, excite, encourage, cause.*'

Curtis smiles. It's a nice smile, one that once must have once got him that extra scoop of ice-cream – and later on, just scoops.

'I'm having you on, laddie – I'm a journo, remember, born with printer's ink under my nails. No, if anyone caused the problem it was Red Robin. It was his style to cause trouble, which was why he was called *Red* …'

There's more of the same but I stopped listening when Curtis upended his glass. There was a lot in it – what he was saying, as well as the glass.

'Okay, I've got a story for you,' I say finally. 'But before I tell you, who hated Cock Robin enough to kill him?'

Curtis takes a swill and this time it's a real swill. He nods like he's come to a decision. 'This is strictly off the record,' he warns. 'If anyone asks, I didn't tell you. Do I have your word on that?'

I tell him *Yeah* and he holds out his hand and I hold out mine and our hands miss but he still takes it for a gentleman's handshake in an era when there aren't any gentlemen. Then he lowers his voice because this is confession time and what he's about to say needs to stay in the confessional.

'I can't name names but my guess is it was someone in the industry.'

'That's it?'

Curtis touches the side of his nose. He might be trying to pick it or it might be a sign. I take it as a sign.

He rubs his shaven head and considers me.

'You're a detective – you work out the rest. Now tell me *your* story.'

I tell him a story.

A unionist's death can be swept under the carpet but kill a cop and the world turns upside down. I tell Minnie and Tsunami to keep a low profile while I keep myself to myself – no swims at Bondi, no trips to Harry's caff, no drinks at the speakeasy. Queen delivers my breakfast and I accept it without demur. I keep my boat clean and my nose cleaner. If my profile was any lower I'd be dead. The world spins on its axis but I don't spin with it. Call me quiet or don't call me at all.

I make a few calls but my ex-girlfriend Annie and my ex-mate Rory won't give me the time of day. I accept the usual rebuffs from my ex-wife Salina when I ask to speak to the kid. I call Aunt Rube but it's like communing with the dead. Finally there's the inevitable lull in the newsworthiness of the cop killing and it's time to return to being a telephone repairman. People nod as they pass. I get to know Mary with the cocker spaniel, the geezer in the Walk-a-Chair, and the postman. I'm a technician in a grey combination overall with writing on it on a street corner in Bondi and most of the telephone conversations are about as exciting as beached eels.

Von Franck's secretary to girlfriend: *She's having an affair behind his back – can you believe it?*
Why, that's terrible!

Yes, isn't it? But understandable under the circumstances ...

Another call and more exclamation marks – this time courtesy of Mrs von Franck.

Yes, of course we'd love to come to dinner! Your place at eight? Should I bring anything? Just Ivan? Doubt enters the voice. *I'll see what I can do ...*

Later, another call from the wife:

I'm sorry but Ivan can't make it. Do you still want me to come? Shall I bring anything? Just myself? I'll see you on Friday ...

I note the day, time and details in my logbook. But what I note most of all are the clicks on the line that tell me someone else apart from me is bugging von Franck.

When you're on a boat, the world's reduced to a narrow compass – the turn of the tide, ships that pass in the night and passing thoughts. Curtis's words churn in my brain: *You're a detective – you work out the rest.* What was he referring to – and why? If it was the occupation of Cock Robin's killer, so what? The pink phone rings. I click on. In the background, the baby's crying, while in the foreground, Tsunami's screaming.

'Calm down,' I say, 'and tell me what's going on.' To hell with confidentiality. 'And this time without the wisteria.'

Tsunami takes a deep breath. The newspapers, television – even the social media – have got their knickers in a knot over Richardson. No-one liked him when he was alive but he was a cop and now that he's dead the cops have to solve his killing. It doesn't matter who they pin it on, as long as they pin it.

'I went to Minnie's to pick up more baby things but couldn't even make it to the door because of the cops. So I left – but not before I saw them with the – what's it called?'

'Shadow board.'

'That's right, the shadow board. Anyway, they're serious now. They're after Minnie and it's only a matter of time before they find her.' There's a significant pause. 'There's something I didn't tell you. I –'

It's time to postpone the dialogue. 'Hold that thought, Tsunami – I'll be right over.'

When I get to Tsunami's, pools of sunlight are strewn on the floorboards like autumn leaves. Tsunami shuffles into the room in espadrilles. That's when I see the resemblance and also what she didn't tell me. But I ask anyway.

'So what didn't you tell me?'

'It – it was no coincidence I met Minnie because I was lying in wait for her. They say a man's good dies with him but there was never any good in Cock Robin. Some people are born bad and there's nothing anyone can do about it. Cock Robin started life as *Little Robbie*, became *That Little Bastard*,

then – because he was adept with a bow and arrow
– *Robin Hood*. Until finally, because he was a cocky
little bastard, he became *Cock Robin*.' Pause. 'He
bashed me until I learnt to fight back. That was what
gave me my taste for the Army. Then I discovered
Minnie was copping it and I had to protect her.'

'You mean … '

'That's right, he was my brother.'

Chapter 36

THE CANARY IN THE MINE

This either sheds new light on the killings or no light at all.

'Why do you feel this information is important now?'

'Because the cops are after Minnie and she's here. And now they're investigating in earnest they're sure to come up with the fact that Robin had a sister and they'll find out where I live. And when they do, they'll have their killer on a plate – even if she didn't do it.'

The two dames and the babe have become a responsibility. They're no longer a way of forgetting my problems – they've become problems themselves. Skinny Minnie and the babe look like The Pieta and Tsunami needs help.

'I think I've worked out who killed Cock Robin and the photographer,' I say. 'But I've got to make it stick. Meanwhile, you're spot on – the cops will find you and, through you, they'll find Minnie. Which means you'll have to go somewhere they won't find you in a hurry ...'

The spider's in his parlour and it's the long-legged variety that wraps up flies and parks them in its web to eat at leisure. Which is why I feel vulnerable when I tell the dame I've come to see Clean Fill. She gives me an unwelcoming smile.

'He's not in.'

'So I'll wait in his office till he gets back.'

She gets the sort of look on her face that people get when things are moving in the opposite direction to the one they want and reaches under the desk. I could stand around waiting but if I do that long enough, Clean Fill will leave via the tradesmen's exit, so instead I step past the dame and throw open the door to find Clean Fill already climbing out of his comfort zone. He reseats himself like he wasn't really thinking of going anywhere. He's still carrying the scars of the fight – a black eye, swollen lip, political embarrassment.

'Nice to see you,' he says.

'Can't say the same.'

'It's still nice to see you,' he repeats. 'How can I help?'

I shut the door. 'By keeping a couple of friends of mine out of the meatworks.'

Clean Fill reaches for the telephone. 'If you don't leave immediately,' he says, 'I'll tell the police.'

'And what will you tell them? That someone's accusing you of the murder of a unionist and a photographer?' His hand comes off the phone and a wary look comes into his eyes. 'I don't know what your game is, O'Hare' – I use his real name, it sounds official – 'but I've got a fair idea. It's called *Making Money* – you go round and round the merry-go-round with a bunch of crooks and the one that ends up with the most dough wins. But your first problem is that I'm not interested in money.'

'And what's my second problem?'

'How you're going to get out of this. My bet is you'll go for the trifecta and play me in with the dames.' Clean Fill looks relieved; I like it when people look relieved – it's called narrowing the field of inquiry. 'Where were you the night Cock Robin copped it?'

The politician recovers his equilibrium, along with a little black book with *APPOINTMENTS* inscribed on the cover in gold. 'I'll need a date and time,' he says.

I give him a date and time and after he flips through his little black book he comes to a page that makes him smile. It's not a nice smile, more like the rictus you find on corpses. He fingers a little badge that reminds him he's been honoured by prosperity.

'I'm sorry to disappoint you, but I have what you might call a *cast-iron alibi*. The day in question was my daughter's birthday and I was helping her celebrate.'

Clean Fill's still smiling as I leave. It doesn't mean much. Or maybe it means everything.

'Happy birthday,' I tell his daughter as I pass.

She smiles her unhappy smile. 'It's not my birthday.'

I take a cab and the circuitous route via The Hills

to lose any tails I might have picked up, either courtesy of the cops or in remembrance of things past. The telephone hydrant's where I left it – a grey protuberance with nice views of the sea – and when I park myself back in the bus shelter wearing the two headphones – one for the phone, the other for the bug I installed at von Franck's the night me and Tsunami paid our visit – it's like listening to sounds in a conch shell. I hear noises that might be the sound of waves, except they're accompanied by too many clicks. Followed by:

Mrs von Franck: *I'm sorry, Maisie, but Ivan still can't come.*

Maisie: *What a shame. But what could be more important than me?*

Mrs von Franck: *I have to be honest with you, I don't know. He'll either sit around doing crosswords or be off on one of his walks with Sherlock – sorry, that's his bloodhound. Anyway, it'll be a lot more fun without him ...*

I've put two and two together and come up with a canary, the kind they put down mines to see if people can stay alive when the air's poisoned – and when the canary dies they know that they can't. Nice birds, canaries – they sing and give up their lives for you. The only trouble is that – looked at from the point of view of the bird – you generally end up with a dead canary.

I go and see Annie. She's serving tarts. 'I see you're serving tarts,' I say by way of conversation.

'Speaking of which,' Annie says, 'You didn't bring yours with you this time, the one with the big, you know – tickets on herself.'

'She's just an acquaintance, Annie.'

Annie smiles, only it's not a nice smile. 'Just like these are just tarts,' she murmurs.

By the time the Mercedes rolls out of von Franck's – the silver one that runs on fifty-dollar bills as opposed to the husband's, which is still in the garage and prefers C-notes – I'm positioned in the shadow of the stink chimney, the one that vents methane from the raw sewage piped out to sea. It must be the guards' night off because I can't see them, which means von Franck must be all alone in his mansion with his dog, himself and his money.

Chapter 37

WHERE THERE'S A WILL ...

I've trawled through his past – backwards, sideways, upwards and downwards – and come up with all the disclaimers. Von Franck arrived in Australia with nothing but that coin: a single, solitary *ban* – which he was at pains to show me he still possesses – starting out as a mortician's assistant and quickly becoming the principal of *FRANK FUNERALS*. Nice name and even nicer business. Von Franck perfected the simple send-off and business prospered.

Meanwhile, his private life – again according to my sources – was what might be called *interesting*. He had a lot of relationships with a lot of dames that were famous and a lot of dames that weren't, blonde and not so blonde, beautiful and not so beautiful. I'll say this for him, he didn't discriminate. Then he met and married the woman that's just gone out to a card game and became a builder – making an even bigger fortune than he had already. Along the way there were the usual *contretemps* but that's the way it is in Sydney – ordinary people like lying on the beach and talking down anyone who doesn't.

I stay glued to the stink chimney.

Von Franck still doesn't go out.

I feel like a ferret at the wrong hole. What if the burrow's empty and the rabbit's in the next warren but one? But the Mercedes is still in the garage and von Franck's hardly likely to have clambered down the cliff. It's cold – which means there's a temperature inversion – and the chimney stinks.

Von Franck killed Cock Robin – that's the view according to Minnie. He had good reason to hate Cock Robin and – with or without the help of either his guards or Clean Fill or both – he also had the motive to frame the victim's widow. The fact that Richardson wanted it otherwise would have played into von Franck's hands. It should have been: *Exit, widow, in direction of Long Bay Jail.* All very neat – too neat. Because it doesn't explain where Clean Fill fits into the picture or why the photographer copped it. Nor does it explain the clicks on von Franck's phone.

Von Franck still doesn't go out.

Solving a case is a matter of discounting prejudices. In the Laboratory Case, where the snake ate the rats, I figured I was pointed in one direction, while what really happened occurred in the house next door. What if von Franck and/or Clean Fill *didn't* kill Cock Robin and are also innocent of killing the photographer – what then? All our technology and the best we can come up with is shit in the sea.

A figure detaches itself from the chimney and for a moment is silhouetted against the night sky. It's either Pandora or someone else. Von Franck still doesn't go out. I abandon the surveil and go back to the boat.

Murder most fowl. When I was a kid, Aunt Rube used to trot out that term and afterwards I'd have nightmares about dead hens. And while the modus operandi varied – the killer might be a fox, a man with an axe or a dog – the result was always the same: there'd be a lot of dead chooks and I'd wake up screaming.

'Murder most foul,' Tsunami's saying now. 'There's no TV in the caravan but the kid wouldn't sleep so I was doing the social media thing when the news went viral.'

The Balmain house is crawling with cops but Tsunami and Minnie are holed up in the van. I'm visiting to make sure they're all right, only to find that – while Minnie and the kid are asleep – Tsunami's as agitated as hell.

Clean Fill was alone in his office when the killer struck. Neighbours heard raised voices but didn't come to investigate. Police described the scene as one of carnage. The photographer's death wasn't worth developing but the cops have linked Clean Fill's with that of Cock Robin and also of Richardson, which means it's gone straight to the darkroom. The latest killing has thrown my theory – that Clean Fill was the murderer – into a cocked hat.

Suddenly I find it hard to breathe. I throw open the door and stumble outside to find the predawn drenching the leaves with dew and the rising sun a threat. I reach into my pocket and feel the coin I found at Clean Fill's; I also feel the cops breathing down my neck.

Tsunami appears behind me. 'If they find evidence linking the deaths,' she asks, 'won't that put Minnie in the clear?'

'Unless they're madmen, murderers kill for a reason. That reason might be money, fear, hatred or revenge. So tell me this: why would someone go out of their way to kill your brother?'

'It wouldn't have been money because he didn't have any – he spent everything he had on what idiots always spend their money on: fast cars, even faster women, drugs and gambling. He was feared but there wasn't all that much fear; and while he was hated, he wasn't all that hated.' She glances past me at the sunrise. 'So by your reckoning, that leaves *revenge …*'

'*A dish best served cold*, just like this case is getting.' I know the answer but I still ask. 'So do you know anyone that felt vengeful towards your brother?'

'I can't think of anyone who didn't.'

The baby starts crying and as Tsunami heads back to the caravan I tell myself that asking people leading questions limits their imagination – ask why they hated their mother and the question assumes the answer. I follow Tsunami back inside – Skinny Minnie's there but she's not there.

'There are now four victims – Cock Robin, the cop, the photographer and the politician. And the cops are saying at least three of them are linked.' I'm thinking aloud. 'We know they're the wrong three but we still know there are three: Cock Robin, the photographer and Clean Fill. If we believe the cops, what's the common factor in those three deaths?'

Tsunami thinks aloud, too. 'Ivan von Franck.'

I'm back listening to bugs. Bugs have an ambient noise – cicadas chatter, flies buzz, mosquitoes whine and the one on von Franck's phone clicks. Why is someone else besides me bugging von Franck? More importantly – who? It could be a rival, the cops, or just someone who …

Click.

Mrs von Franck: *Thanks for the other night, I did enjoy myself. Frankie can be so sullen. His public image might be rosy but that's not the way he is at home. I sometimes wish …*

Maisie: *But that's just what we were saying when you were here, isn't it? The more money there is, the more misery …*

Mrs von Franck: *Yes, but murder?*

Silence, apart from a flurry of clicks. Then:

Maisie: *What do you mean?*

Mrs von Franck: *Oh, Maisie, I have to tell someone. You know how Ivan's not interested in me any more? Do you think there's another woman – a woman he's serious about? And could it be linked to these deaths? Does that mean I might be next?*

Maisie: *Sheila!*

Mrs von Franck: *What am I going to do?*

Maisie: *You can pull yourself together for a start. Because if you leave him you won't get anything …*

Mrs von Franck: *But if I stay I could be next. Is money worth dying for?*

Maisie: *If there's enough of it. I'm only joking, Sheila. Seriously, though, is there a will? Remember where there's a will there's a way. I think you should see a lawyer …*

I find Curtis in the pub.

'I need your newspaper's files on von Franck.'

The light shines off his head while the chatter of the other journalists ebbs and flows around us like hot air out of a hairdrier. I could go to Wackipedia but all it's going to tell me is that von Franck's successful and likes the ladies and I already know that. Except that Wackipedia might give me a clue as to *which* lady …

'Electronic or solid?' Curtis says at last. 'Let me explain. Newspaper libraries used to be known as *morgues.*' He raises his glass and this time he drinks from it. 'That was because they were places where articles went to die. You see, journalism's got a very short shelf life. Once they're published, stories are no more than corpses, doing what corpses do – turning yellow and rotting. But that was in the old days – modern records are computerised. Which ones do you want?'

'Both.'

Curtis demolishes the rest of his beer. In the time I've known him, he's never done that. Like any good journo, he'll sip or he'll knock his glass over but he'll always stay sober – even while he's busy pretending to be as drunk as a monk. A pokie next door goes *ker-chunk* and Curtis comes to a decision.

'All right, why not?'

Chapter 38

... THERE'S A WAY

The computerised files – that is, the ones on the memory stick – get me back as far as the 1980s, when newspapers switched from the clunky past to sweeping modernity, and I need to go beyond that. But apart from the memory stick, Curtis also gave me a mountain of yellowing newspaper clippings in a lot of dusty manila folders contained in what used to be brown and called a *kitbag* but is now bright yellow and rebadged *stuff sack*. He handed me the yellow sack – together with the USB – in Hyde Park where there was no-one to witness the transaction – no-one, that is, apart from the two shadows behind the Moreton Bay fig, a couple of trees down from the War Memorial.

'I didn't give you this,' he says, glancing around. 'It fell off the back of a truck when the driver wasn't looking. I won't ask what you're after but I assume it's to do with the murders. I'll need it back. Few people worry about old-time newspaper morgues any more but it's the principle …'

'Thanks.'

'Don't mention it. And I mean that.'

I know I'm being followed because – after crossing Elizabeth Street and heading along Park before turning down George by the Woolworths Building then right into Chinatown, after which I double back towards the Semi-circular Quay – they're still there: the two that broke Mismatch's arm, thumped me outside the politician's office and later turned up as guards at von Franck's. I duck into the Queen Victoria Building and telephone Tsunami from Victoria's Basement.

'Where are you?' I ask.

'At work – I need a break from that bloody kid.'

'I've got a job for you, Tsunami.'

'What kind of job?'

'A decoy job. You'll need to dress up for it.'

'Do I get shot at?'

'Not necessarily.'

Pause. It's a soldier's pause, the kind that soldiers make before accepting a mission they suspect might end in their death. 'What do you want me to do?'

I tell her what I want her to do and after she chews it over for a moment, she's prepared to oblige. Not happy, just prepared to oblige. I click off, disentangle myself from the shop's cut-price saucepan section and head back towards Central Railway Station, and the only old-time army disposal store the developers have left standing.

It's late afternoon by the time I meet Tsunami on the corner of Sussex and Park. I've taken the long way round to shake the tail and I'm wearing army-surplus jungle greens and carrying two bags – both apparently full: one brown, the other yellow – and Tsunami's wearing pretty much what I had on before I changed: a bright red coat, blue strides, trainers that from a distance look like my whitesides, and a hat pulled down over her short-cropped hair.

'Where did you get the clothes?'

My doppelganger shrugs. She's even got the shrug right.

'I bought them at one of those pop-up shops. I asked for the worst clothes they had and ended up looking like you.'

'Give me your phone and take this one.' I switch on the pink phone and hand it to her. 'They'll have tabs on it so they'll pick you up in less than a minute, but as long as you stay in full public view you'll be safe. Stay away from nooks and crannies and keep walking. Meanwhile, I've got some homework to do. I'll call you when I'm done.'

I stay in the Limited News doorway on Park as Tsunami swaggers off towards the Cross, doing a more than fair imitation of my walk. She's carrying the yellow bag and she's bulked out her shoulders and the hat and the coat and the way she's walking do the rest. If I wasn't me I'd swear that she was. On cue, the thugs who witnessed the transaction between me and the pilgarlic fall into step behind her.

As long as they think she's me they'll be careful to stay where she won't see them and also not try anything on until they're certain they won't be seen. Which means that as long as Tsunami does what I told her, she won't get hurt. I board a bus, get off at Cammeray, hoof it to the shore, turn the coracle right side up, put the brown kitbag in the stern, push the boat into the water, and row out to the *Wooden No*.

Dusk is clamping its iron fist over the mouth of the Harbour and the brown bag is a veritable Pandora's Box. A boat drifts past making the *Wooden No* rock at her mooring, swirling in the bigger vessel's whirlpools. I make out the distinctive superstructure of what must be von Franck's boat, bigger than death and even more stupefying, and as I stare through the porthole, plague flies and disease-bearing mosquitoes fill the cabin.

Everywhere I look cries out von Franck: the city skyline's von Franck; a billboard on North Sydney's highest tower says *BLUEBIRD ENTERPRISES*; the deaths are linked to von Franck; and the files in the sack on the chart table are full of him — file after dusty file going back decades. I drag the laptop out of the sail locker, plug it into the 240-volt outlet, switch on and insert the thumb drive in the port featuring the *menorah*.

The gun's uncomfortable so I remove it, placing it on the map table next to the files. If von Franck ever did anything wrong, you didn't read it in the *Terrorgraph*. Because for years Curtis has not only been covering industrial rounds, he's also been covering for von Franck. The memory stick takes me back to 1987 but that's not far enough so I switch my attention to the *stuff sack*.

A heading in *The Sydney Morning Horrible* says: *WILL THIS BE THE WORLD'S FIRST CONDEMNED SKYSCRAPER?* And the story starts: *So far investigators have found 137 faults in the tower …* I flick through the rest of the files.

The movie Aunt Rube screened on the wall of my childhood almost as often as the Jimmy Cagney gangster flicks was the 1930s creak-and-groan monster classic, *Frankenstein*. It was all about thunder and lightning, dark nights, lonely moors and a mad scientist's slash-and-burn laboratory. Legs and arms, a head, eye of toad, leg of newt. *Why am I showing you this?* Rube would ask. *Because you're as mad as a mashed potato,* I'd reply – but not out loud. *Because you want to frighten a little orphan boy half to death, because you're a crazy old spinster with nothing better to do than show scary movies to kids …* A scientist created life out of death and thought he was God. Except that the life he created was a monster. *Why am I showing you this?* Rube would repeat. *Because you're bloody insane!* I replied to myself. But all I said out loud was: *I dunno.*

Then think about it, Rube would say. *Because there's a reason …*

Chapter 39

HERD IT ALL BEFORE

There's a reason for von Franck, too. He was a poor little immigrant boy who found refuge in Australia and struck it rich. Like the monster in the movie, he was born fully grown. There was another birth thirty years before but that didn't count because his real birth was in Australia in the early 1980s. That's when the media discovered him so it's when he was born. The birth notice appeared in the *Terrorgraph*, accompanied by a photo of a thirty-year-old man flipping a coin.

NO BAN TO SUCCESS
Ivan von Franck grew up in the shadow of death. Romania's Ceausescu regime killed off his parents, sister, aunts, cousins, friends – a start in life that would have destroyed a lesser man.

But since finding sanctuary in Australia, Ivan von Franck has forged a meteorically successful career. In just a few short years, Frank Funerals became synonymous with death. Then von Franck branched out into building. He's just landed a major government contract. We asked Ivan von Franck a few questions.

(Here the journalist adopts a pose of wide-eyed astonishment.)

JOURNALIST: Mr von Franck, from graves to

building in a single bound!

VON FRANCK (flipping his trademark coin): What's the surprise? Building's just another hole in the ground that needs filling. That makes it the same as burying, but without the grief.

JOURNALIST: So tell me about that coin.

VON FRANCK: It's all I came to this country with — a 1952 Romanian penny, what they call a ban — that's not a green ban, by the way! No more than a gram of cupronickel but to me a symbol of my success.

There's more of the sycophantic same — too much more. *That's von Franck, the story winds up, an enigma wrapped in a puzzle who only answers questions with more questions. And why not? The only thing not to query, in this humble reporter's opinion, is that von Franck will reach the stars he's so clearly aiming for.*

The story's a set piece where the journalist asks questions the interviewee wants to be asked. It's called *absentee journalism* because journalist appears to be absent. And the name at the end is …

So the two go back that far. I skim through the rest of the files and von Franck's life's like a movie in which a plant grows at lightning speed. A shoot pops out of the ground and takes a look around, leaves appear, there's a bud, the bud unfolds, and suddenly, lo and behold! — there's a flower. Media-born in 1982, by 2014 von Franck's a rip-roaring success. One of the mobiles rings. I click on.

'Brownie?'

'Yeah?'

'They're closing in.' It's a voice from a war zone. 'I

feel like a sheep being herded by a pair of kelpies.'

'Where are you?'

'Where you and I were before, at von Franck's project. I don't know if I was aiming for it or if my followers herded me here.' The old *herd-it-all-before* trick. 'I thought it was a through road but it turns out to be a dead end. They bury people on building sites, don't they?'

'Can you get inside the building?'

'I think that's what they want me to do.'

'Is there anywhere else to go?'

There's a pause, during which I hear the sounds of the city – the revving of engines, horns blaring, the whisper of footsteps. Tsunami comes back on the phone.

'No,' she whispers.

'Then you've got no choice. As an engineer, you'd know your way around construction sites, while the chances are your followers don't.'

'Okay.'

'Stay alert and stay alive.' I get myself up on deck. 'Hold them off as long as you can. Chuck that bagful of nothing at them if that's all you've got. But get in that building and start climbing. I'll be there as soon as I can.'

I'm halfway to shore before I remember the gun. It's still on the map table beside the stuff sack. I've got the folder but I forgot the gun. Only it's too late to turn back.

I row to shore, beach the coracle and hoof it to the shops, where I flag a cab. Using my pen torch to study the file as the taxi weaves through the North Sydney traffic before crossing the Bridge, I learn how von Franck's life reconstructed itself like a skyscraper, story upon story. Cuttings files consist of articles that have been dated, arranged according to subject matter, pasted onto sheets of A4 paper, and filed. I riffle through 1985, 1984, 1983 – there are white spaces where cuttings have been removed from their backing sheets but otherwise it's all yellowing newsprint: von Franck in front of his third tower, his second, his first; coloured pictures from women's magazines: von Franck squiring a beautiful blonde; von Franck with a brunette; von Franck with … The cab hits a bump and a picture slides out from behind another one – unglued, an orphan, and therefore overlooked, showing von Franck with yet another dame, a dame who's gazing up at him adoringly; a dame that's somehow familiar. I remove the picture and slip it in my pocket.

I pay the cabbie, open the door and get out, keeping the photo but leaving the rest of the folder in the cab. It'll find its way back to where it belongs. The phone rings again like it never stopped ringing. I click on.

'Where are you, Brownie?'

'Where are *you*?'

'Where you told me to be, up the tower.'

'How did you get onto the site?'

'Like any good soldier, over the top of the hoarding.'

'Where are your followers?'

Chapter 40

A VOID DANGER

Why do you think I'm showing you this movie? Rube would ask. *I dunno,* I'd reply.

'They can't be far off, Brownie,' Tsunami says.

'Stay away from the edge.'

I start running.

Somewhere there's a blue bird of happiness ... The words are from a song and the song's from a play by a joker called Maeterlinck who believed happiness comes from within. Clearly he didn't have much of a hold on reality. *Why do you think I'm showing you this movie?* Rube would ask. *Who do you think is the monster?* Finally she answered her own question: *The monster's in all of us, Rainbow – we're the monster ...*

I'm in front of the big, wide door that – when things are running smoothly – provides access for trucks. But the trucks are idle, the signs say *KEEP OUT – NO ENTRY* and the door is locked. A sign reads *A VOID DANGER*. It's got a concrete base and in normal circumstances I wouldn't be able to move it. But these circumstances aren't normal. I pick up the sign, swing it around my head, let go on the turn – and the gate is suddenly splinters. The roadway slopes down to the building site, its surface scarred by trucks. I slide into the abyss, prop, look up.

Three hundred metres is nearly a third of a kilometre and that's how high the building's framework is, the top floor too far away to see it. I seek and locate the unclad building's backbone – the lift well, its bank of buttons glowing blue. I hit the *Up* button and a mechanical voice says: *Enter*. I do like the voice says and after entering turn and face outwards, just in time to see a shadow – or is it two shadows? – move across my field of vision. It might be my imagination. Then again it mightn't.

The doors close and, apart from the blue-lit buttons, I'm in darkness. The lift's padded because during construction it carries building materials and when it moves it's with the grace of a wounded alligator. Now and again there's a lurch and a scraping sound like a grounded vessel trying to free itself from a reef. I hear a sound that could be that of another lift but it might be my imagination.

A cold wind slams into me as I step out onto the rooftop. Dull halogens illuminate the roof while, halfway along the bank of lifts, I make out what looks like the feeble gleam of another torch. The torch – if it *is* a torch and not an aeroplane or a star – stays still for five, maybe six seconds before moving on again. There's no sign of Tsunami but I didn't expect any. She would have heard the lift and decided it must be the tail. The light over the lifts flickers and goes out.

Hard hats, high-vis jackets and building materials – tiles, tins, bags, timber and steel mesh – are heaped about indiscriminately. A frayed length of rope – there's not much life left in it – is coiled loosely around a battered wheelbarrow while a couple of portable toilets are parked near a stack of bricks, the rope end winding aimlessly between them. The safety fence is little more than knee-high, propped up by star posts. There's concrete, then there's no concrete – nothingness ending in the glittering fireflies of office buildings across the road and, far below, the slow-moving headlights of toy cars. A crane stands idle, its hook dangling like the noose of a gallows.

At three hundred metres, darkness eats light. I step back from the abyss. To my left is the beginning of the stairs and next to them the lifts form a squat, square block against the night sky. I hear footsteps. This is danger time and I'm in it.

Killers don't think like the rest of us. They're wild dogs, focused on one of three things – sleep, the nearest bitch or their prey. These two are the goons from von Franck's. Their shadows split away from the fire escape.

I haven't got my back against the wall because there's no wall to have my back against, just a poor excuse for a safety rail with certain death a third of a kilometre below. The goons are doing what they know to do, splitting up to deprive their prey of a single target, in case there's any fight left in their prey. I hear nothing from the shadows, just note their signals. And after a while, the small figure disappears behind the lifts while the tall one heads directly for me.

This isn't a cat-and-mouse game because there's no hole to hide in. I hear the small thug scuttling behind the liftwell. The torches aren't lasers or Gobi-lights or G3 whizzbangs – just common-and-garden head-mounted lamps. But they're enough. I'm unarmed and Tsunami wouldn't be carrying, either. The halogens bang and fizzle and go out, leaving the rooftop in darkness except for the pinpoint glow of one headlamp. Three hundred metres is too far to jump. There's the rope but that would get me three floors at most before it frayed completely and snapped. And first I've got to find Tsunami.

The Fat Lady's only ten paces away, partly obscured by the bricks. Off to my right, I hear the soft-shoe shuffle of the small thug, Lofty, as he approaches. If I move my head slightly I can see the stairs, the lifts, assorted junk, the barrow and the dangling hook of the crane – but no Tsunami.

Chapter 41

IT'S NOT OVER TILL ...

All my guns are on the boat – the three Smith & Wessons, the two Brownings, the Glock, the five Specials – one on the map table while the rest are neatly wrapped in plastic bags and inserted in the fake S-bend of the head, the lavatory. It's not much of a hiding place but, despite what they say in the movies, searchers gloss over dunnies.

That's when the penny or the pfennig or in von Franck's case, the *ban*, drops. Tsunami's in one of the Port-a-loos because there's nowhere else to hide. Before long the goons will kill me and after that they'll work out where Tsunami is and kill her, too.

I've got to think like them, put myself in their Nikes and put it fast. Don Bradman's got a bat while the Fat Lady's carrying a Uzi. I've worked out where Tsunami is but I'm behind the bricks and the 8-ball. *Think like them*, I tell myself, *they're after a kill – which means I've got to provide them with one.* I hear the building creak. Then I realise it's not the building at all but a lavatory door opening. The rope's loose-coiled between me and the Fat Lady and the barrow's on top of the coil. The dunny door swings open and I reach for the end of the rope ...

Animals react to whatever makes the greatest movement. A dog will take on a rampaging bull rather than a mouse because the bull's bigger and therefore poses the greater threat. The Fat Lady's got a choice between a squeaking door and a barrow that suddenly rears towards her. She ignores the door and takes out the barrow.

It doesn't take long to empty a 32-round magazine at a cyclic rate of 1900 revolutions per minute and that's how long it takes the Fat Lady to turn the barrow into a sieve. There's the familiar clatter-click as she replaces the empty magazine with a full one. Tsunami's still got the yellow fun bag like it contains the crown jewels instead of a lot of wadded-up newspaper, and together with the red coat, the hat and the daks she's a beacon. I reach out, grab her and drag her behind the bricks. I haven't got any tricks left and now they know where we are.

'Wha –' she starts.

She's interrupted by another burst from the Uzi that sends brick fragments flying over our heads.

'Take off the jacket!' I whisper.

Lofty's coming down one side of the rooftop while the Fat Lady's coming along the other. Tsunami shrugs herself out of the jacket and hands it to me as another magazineful of slugs unleashes itself into the bricks. I count thirty-two then chuck the coat. It lands on the hook of the crane and the beam of the Fat Lady's lamp swings around to greet it. She sees the red coat and remembers that's what she's here to kill. She changes magazines. Then she kills the coat.

The brick's heavy but I learnt to dance with bricks, pirouetting with one in each hand in order to develop the requisite poise, strength and balance for ballet. I bring my arm back and step out from behind the bricks. I'm throwing blind but I'm rewarded with a scream that doesn't hang around and a bat skittering across concrete. I figure Lofty's gone over the edge but there's still the Fat Lady and she's the danger man. Another magazine clicks into place.

'Come out,' the Fat Lady orders.

Beside me, I feel Tsunami shiver. 'We're going to die, aren't we, Brownie?' she whispers.

I shake my head. 'Like they say in the classics, it's not over till the Fat Lady sings.'

I can't see the Fat Lady but I know where she is by where all the grunts are coming from: primordial noises, the sound a fox makes on a lonely hillside at night or a dingo makes as it moves in for the kill. *Confronted by a wild dog, you have to put yourself in its place,* Rube used to say. *Which means you need to react like a wild dog.*

But if I'm going to die, I'm going to die rational. If I die it's got to be for a reason and right now that reason's Tsunami. There's no such thing as luck, no *force majeure* appearing out of nowhere when the crisps are down. Fortune á la Rube: *You need to make your own luck in this world, Rainbow.*

The Fat Lady's only three paces away and she's got the Uzi lying along the *radius* and *ulna* of her left arm with thirty-two nice, bright, shiny new rounds in the magazine. The first and second phalanxes of her index finger are tucked inside the trigger guard and death – our death: mine and Tsunami's – is imminent. She's stopped speaking because cunning's cut in – she knows that any noise she makes now will give away her position.

We could be hiding from a spectre, a ghost, a shroud, a miasma. Tsunami huddles in close, shivering like a featherless bird. The world's suddenly gone quiet because the hunter's suddenly gone smart. A crocodile lies as still as a floating log as it awaits its prey and a spider hangs immobile in its web. I've created a diversion but all that's done is told the Fat Lady where we are. I replay the snapshot of what I saw last: the top of the liftwell, the pile of bricks, the lime and mortar, the barrow that's now a sieve, a length of rope, a shot-up coat, the cricket bat. I could chuck another brick but this time the Fat Lady will be ready and close in for the kill. The cricket bat …

There was nothing to stop Lofty going over the edge – from the sound the brick made when it struck it was a skull-shot. I do the physiology. At the moment of impact, all tension leaves the body. It's like a baby falling – the muscles and ligaments turn to cheese, knees relax, toes unclench, the arms fly out in a *post impressione* gesture as the body's forced backwards while the fingers unclench from whatever they're gripping.

But a bat's not part of the physiology. So what happened to the bat? I remember the *twang* as the fence snapped which told me Lofty must have gone over. But what happened to the bat?

I ease a brick out of the stack like I'm removing a slug from a still-beating heart, hand it to Tsunami and indicate by dumb show where she's to throw it – afterwards miming a *rat-a-tat-tat* to remind her the Fat Lady's armed. Tsunami nods and when I hold up my hand, fingers spread, she understands that, too. Five seconds to go and the countdown starts – *now!*

I'm holding the hand up on the turn, folding one finger down as I go: *One!* I step to the other end of the pile and another finger comes down: *Two!* I locate the bat, black against the moon-white cement: *Three!* I visualise grabbing the bat and swinging it: *Four!* I glance behind me – Tsunami's already bringing her brick arm forward as I dive, grab, swivel and swing: *Five!*

I hear the brick rattle and roll followed by the *rat-a-tat-tat* of the gat. But two things happen that aren't supposed to happen – the machine-gun burst isn't long enough and Lofty's got hold of my leg because he didn't go over the edge at all and by the time I'm within swinging distance of the Fat Lady, Lofty's hand's attached to my ankle like a limpet and the

Fat Lady's swinging the snout of the Uzi towards me and I know it's still got bullets in it because I counted and …

I've got the bat but the Fat Lady's got the gun and it's aimed at my head and I'm done for. But Tsunami isn't. I see her rise up behind the Fat Lady and she might be unarmed but she's got surprise on her side, as well as a sound knowledge of unarmed combat, and the cutting edge of her hand catches the Fat Lady on the side of the neck, the headlamp goes flying and the Fat Lady goes down. I give Lofty a whack with the bat and he goes sleepy-byes.

Tsunami finishes wrapping up the small man with some twine she's found and is retrieving the headlamp as I secure the Fat Lady's legs with the rope. Tsunami shines the lamp in the Fat Lady's face as she comes round and her pupils roll like a pair of dice as they take in her surrounds – her trussed-up mate, the bricks, the barrow, Tsunami and the rope.

'Where's von Franck?' I ask.

'Don't tell him!' It's Lofty, awake and straining against his bonds; his voice is as squeaky as the Port-a-loo door but I can still make out what he says. 'The bastard hasn't killed us yet which means the chances are that he won't; you don't have to say nothing.'

The Fat Lady looks at Lofty with contempt; it's been a long time coming, this contempt, probably a lifetime. 'Your logic's not even as good as your English, little man,' she says. 'Don't you see? If I don't tell him what he wants to know, we're dead; but if I do tell him, we've still got a chance.'

Chapter 42

... THE FAT LADY SWINGS

A look passes between them and it's not a nice look. There's something happening here and I'm not sure what it is. But what I *do* know is that Cock Robin's dead; after that the photographer; then the politician – not to mention the cop – and me and Tsunami were supposed to be the follow-up act.

'There's been enough deaths,' I say. 'So where is he?'

'What will you do with us after I tell you?'

'This ain't a debate.'

'You'll hand us over to the cops, won't you?'

'Come on, you're a couple of standover merchants that have had their day – the cops have got better things to do with their time than bother about you, unless you're the killers: like extortion, drug-filching and general mayhem. Where is he?'

'He's …' she begins.

'Don't tell them!' Lofty shouts.

The Fat Lady shrugs; she looks defeated.

'I have to tell him, Lofty.'

'No, you don't, Bruce, you –!'

For a moment the Fat Lady reminded me of Madam Blavatsky but that was before Lofty said what he just said. In the light of Tsunami's torch I examine the Fat Lady more closely and when I do I see what I should have seen all along – that the Fat Lady's waist is too low and the hips are too narrow and that she's shaped like an inverted triangle instead of an approximation of an hourglass. The Fat Lady's not only not fat she's not even a lady. But what does that mean except that people are tricky with names? And what does it matter anyway? Because what matters is –

'Who's Lofty so afraid of?'

The Fat Lady shakes her head – either in the negative, or just to clear it.

'It's –'

Killing's like lime milkshakes – once you start, you can't stop. And Death must have been Lofty's constant companion because he knows how it works: after they report failure to whoever they work for, they'll die in our place. It's called clearing the decks and it's what Lofty's about to do as I urge the Fat Lady to finish what he started saying. But if I thought the Fat Lady would sing like a canary, I'm disappointed. He's said something but he hasn't said enough and he could be playing the wrong tune anyway. He wants to live and that's a good sign but it looks like there's zero hope of an encore.

'Who?' I urge.

But it's too late – Lofty launches himself and his head catches the Fat Lady in a place where it hurts because the Fat Lady's no lady and his legs might be trussed but his hands are free and he grabs Lofty and hugging each other they roll together towards the safety fence that isn't a safety fence and they go over, the knot on the end of the rope tied around the Fat Lady catching under the bricks and the rope tightening as, three floors down, the entwined bodies thump against the side of the skyscraper once, twice, three times before the Fat Lady must have realised that, even though he's not fat and his accomplice is only small, their combined weight is still going to be too much for a frayed rope, and as the rope snaps, I hear the Fat Lady's swansong in *diminuendo* as he takes his last dive.

It's not over till the Fat Lady swings.

And the Fat Lady's just swung.

By the light of the lamp I find my coat. It's shot full of holes, just like the case. There's still some material in both, but not enough, not nearly enough, and when I drape the coat around Tsunami's shoulders, it doesn't stop her shivering.

'Who was she talking about? I thought that ...'

Her voice trails away. *You just shot the messenger,* a little bird tells me. *But if the Fat Lady was the messenger, what was the message – and who sent him?* The Cock Robin case started in a scientist's laboratory with an escaped snake, too many dead rats and an eternal triangle, and I saw only what I was meant to see. What I've got to look for now is what I'm *not* meant to see.

The *Wooden No* rocks at her moorings. I've taken

Tsunami back to the caravan where she can look after Skinny Minnie and made the return trip in the cab, the cab driver's voice an annoying murmur: *Look, I know it ain't none of my business but you just dumped a dame in the bush.* And I tell him, *Yeah, you're right, it ain't none of your business …*

A ferry's hooter blasts, sharks fade in and out of rocky crevices, deadly blue-ringed octopuses search for prey and dangerous currents swirl. When we left the building site, two bodies lay smashed. Someone will complain to the coroner: *We warned people it was dangerous by way of obligatory signs that said* A VOID DANGER. And leave it at that.

Except I can't leave it at that. I go over the evidence:

Someone broke into a lab

A unionist was murdered

A photographer was shot

Followed by a politician

And there's only the one clue: *Blue …*

Common factor Number One: Ivan von Franck. Other common factors …

I usually have Rube to bounce things off, or Rory, or Imogene, or Annie. But one by one they've gone over the edge leaving nothing but echoes. Like the cab driver said: *I know it's none of my business but …* Other common factors –

Who are the suspects? *Nine times out of ten it's the wife.* In the case of the lab break-in, everything pointed to the wife – although my money was always on the assistant. With Cock Robin, everyone thought it was the widow while the widow insisted it was von Franck. When the cop died, the finger of suspicion returned to Skinny Minnie, Cock Robin's widow. Then there was the fight and Clean Fill was killed and again von Franck looked to be the guilty party. Except that would be a coincidence and I don't do coincidence. But it must have been someone connected with Cock Robin – or von Franck. There was the death of Clean Fill, immediately following the brawl, and before that the death of the photographer. *Nine times out of ten it's the wife ... Think, dammit, think!*

The scientist was working for von Franck – so could the lab wrecker have been von Franck himself? But if so, why? Because there's always got to be a *why* and where there's a *why* there's a *will. Seriously, though,* von Franck's wife's friend told her: *where there's a will there's a way. I think you should see a lawyer ...*

I'm wearing the coat, the one I wore when I visited Clean Fill and before that, the lab, the one that the Fat Lady who wasn't a fat lady at all shot full of holes, and as a result I'm shivering. But who says my shivering's the fault of the holes? Couldn't I just be shivering because ... What's intuition if not a barbed-wire entanglement made up of prejudices? What if I'm presupposing too much?

What I take to be von Franck's boat sails past, rocking the *Wooden No.* The monster's as big as Fate and, silhouetted against the city skyline, I can make out the funnels – except suddenly I see that they're not funnels at all but the jumble of skyscrapers in the city behind the boat. I bring out the night scope to discover that it isn't even von Franck's boat but one of those cruise ships that takes revellers for jaunts around the harbour. I only *thought* it was von Franck's because that's what I expected to see and I expected to see it because my mind was full of von Franck.

I drop the binoculars and dive back inside to the map table and what's left of the files, the sackful of stories Curtis got me. The answer's been staring me in the face all the time. *There are none so blind as those that will not see,* as Rube would have said. *Or,* she might have added, *as those who were tricked into looking in the other direction.* I go back to the beginning, the year the all-new Ivan von Franck was born. And this time I'm not looking for what I'm supposed to be looking for. Instead I'm looking for the other side of the coin.

Von Franck's wife answers on the tenth ring and I remember Rule One, where all this started – that nine times out of ten it's the wife.

'Mrs von Franck?'

'Yes, this is she. To whom am I speaking?'

I tell her to whom she's speaking and, although it isn't the truth, it'll have to do.

'Look, it's very late,' she says. 'Can't this wait until morning?'

'Not if you want to help your husband,' I reply. 'Do you in fact want to help your husband, Mrs von Franck?'

'Of course I want to help my husband,' she snaps. 'Doesn't every wife?'

'Okay, if you want to help him, tell me where he is.'

'Who did you say you were again?'

I tell her who I said I was again.

'And why do you want to know where he is?'

I tell her it's a matter of life and death; I don't say whose life or whose death; but it seems to satisfy her. 'Well, there *is* one place that comes to mind.'

Chapter 43

GRAVE RUN

It's a two-man operation and Rory's no longer available so I call Vertical. Vertical's a back-up man who's called vertical because something's wrong with one of his legs, so he leans.

'It's 4 a.m. in the bloody morning!' he says.

'Death doesn't wear a wristwatch, Vertical. You got wheels?'

Too right he's got wheels. In fact, he's got a 1956 FJ Holden, beautifully restored, re-ducoed in the original black, with red upholstery, its big spidery steering wheel complete with red-nose horn, white-walled tyres with lion-and-ball hubcaps and a heavily-chromium-plated front grille – a car to die for. I cut across his encomium.

'Spare me the details, Vert, and meet me in North Sydney in half an hour.'

The car's at the kerb. I adjust the Smith & Double-You and climb in.

'There's no air-conditioning so the back windows have to stay open if you want to breathe,' Vertical shouts above the burble of the speared muffler as I scratch around. 'And you can stop looking for a safety belt because there isn't one. This is an old car so belts aren't mandatory and for the same reason there's no headrests or airbags. Where do you want to go?'

'Waverley Cemetery.'

'Why do you need me?'

'To drive the car.'

'I mean after that.'

'For back-up. But we'll cross that bridge when we come to it.'

'You mean the Sydney Harbour Bridge?'

'Yeah, that, too.'

The cemetery's gates are locked and above the burble of the Holden the Tasman is hammering against the cliff like it's demanding entry. Otherwise the place is as quiet as the grave. It figures.

I tell Vertical to park the jalopy in front of the Mercedes, cut the engine and shut up. Plastic flowers perch on sandstone- and marble-covered plots in fond memory of the dear departed. We take the easterly path – down dale and uphill, away from the row of mausoleums and towards the sound of the sea. The graveyard smells of new-mown hay and a pair of lovers is murmuring sweet nothings to one another in the little stone shelter overlooking the Tasman. I give them a wide berth.

'Christ, this is spooky,' Vertical mutters. 'Why can't we do this in the daytime?'

I tell him daytime will be too late. We zig-zag past graves. Stone angels vie for elbow room with marble cupids. Some plots contain nice-tended gardens while others are miniature forests. The moonlight reveals inscriptions rewritten by Time: *PEST IN PEA, WE'LL NEVER FORGE HIM* and *MUCK LOVED BY AL*. *Ivan likes to walk the dog there by moonlight,* von Franck's wife told me. *He says that, given his harsh beginnings, death inspires him.*

She could have been mistaken – she might even have deliberately misled me. Or else von Franck has come and gone – only I don't think that's the case because his Mercedes Benz is still parked by the gates. We complete the round-tour but find nothing but more graves and we're back near the shelter shed to find the lovers are no longer whispering sweet nothings to each other but instead appear to be arguing.

Vertical tugs at my arm. 'This ain't none of our business, Rainbow,' he says. 'So why don't we just clear out and come back in the morning?'

It's hard to make out what the lovers are saying over the noise of the waves. It's like the worn-out R.I.P.s on the headstones – I've got to fill in the gaps made by the elements, try to make sense of what otherwise makes no sense at all, plug the holes where the missing letters and words should be …

Voice 1*: '… It …'*

Voice 2: *'Look, I know we were once* homaláu *but that was long … never ought … you've been … all these … ears …'*

You imagine lovers' voices to be forever young but these ones are old, one angry and the other tinged with sadness, a voice used to negotiating minefields, whatever form they might take, while the other …

Voice 1: *grudge … when someone's … after all these … justice is what …'*

Voice 2 (laughing, but without mirth): *'You're like securitatea … secret police … justice for imagined wrongs … justice when they really meant …'*

Voice 1: *'… real enough …'*

There's two things wrong with this lovers' tiff:

Voice 1 is vengeful while Voice 2 isn't a lover's voice at all but sounds like it wants to walk away, yet for reasons best known to itself is staying. And they're not lovers at all, at least not any more.

The word *revenge* hangs in the air like a shelf of rock after centuries of wind and waves have hammered away at it. I try to see what's under the overhang but all I can make out is darkness. It's not like the *chiaroscuro* of the paintings Aunt Rube failed to get me to understand, vague images of pots and pans and other loose ends under a bed, or a dog by a fire. *Dog? What dog?*

The wind's risen and with it the racket of the waves. Which means not only can I no longer make out many of the words, it's impossible to make out which one's speaking.

Voice: *In … Faustus … the Devil … his due … because … Devil's deal … day of reckoning …*

When someone talks about a day of reckoning – whether it's the prey or the stalker – it's time to act. Because the day of reckoning is settlement day, when people fulfil their destiny and pay their accounts. Like they say in the Litany: *In all the time of our tribulation; in all the time of our wealth; in the hour of death and in the Day of Judgment, Good Lord deliver us …*

Voice: *Nelu, Nelu, nu fi prost …*

I know enough Romanian to know those words mean: *Don't do it!* Which means it's time to do something because neither the Good Lord nor anyone else will be doing anything, unless it's to deliver Death. I haul out the gat and motion Vertical one way while I go the other. But I stumble, the gun flies out of my hand and, after I manage to steady myself and look down to see what I tripped over, I see it's the dog, the bloodhound I silenced at von Franck's all those aeons ago, the one with the tired-looking eyes that will never be tired-looking again because the dog's tongue's lolling out and its eyes are closed forever. It slows me. The death of a dog always slows me. But you can't afford to be slowed in this game and I'm only halfway to the entrance when I hear the shot – in the confines of the shelter it sounds like a cannonade – followed by another, then a shout, then several more shots, followed by silence, apart from the sound of the waves.

The figure's heading up the hill towards the gates, making a transverse section across the graves, a grey shape against the sharp white of the marble pillars, stumbling over ankle-high wrought-iron fences, ricocheting around sandstone angels and racketing along a path before reaching the fresh-cut grass. At least one unburied body – two counting the dog

– lies on the consecrated ground behind us. After all those years of smouldering hatred, Voice 1 has had its revenge. Only it didn't pan out the way it intended, not the way it intended at all.

We're not leaping tall buildings at a single bound but it's something like. It's called *parkourse* or something like it and involves running in a straight line, despite impediments – much like life. The figure vaults over a gargoyle, hurdles a grave plot, swings around a statue that's too high to leap over, and I follow. I've got to catch the figure because if it gets away, the chances of ever pinning anything on it – even several deaths – will be next to impossible.

Revenge is a dish best served cold, the old saying goes, and this particular dish has been years in the making.

Chapter 44

A CAR TO DIE FOR

The Holden's unlocked with the key in the ignition and it starts first go because Vertical's done a nice job on the resto. The gears crunch as the driver wrenches the column lever into reverse and through the gate I see the car back and fill. It's not a clean fill because on the way back it crunches into the front of the Mercedes. I leap the fence as the driver slams the gear lever into first. There are three paces between me and the car and the distance is growing rapidly.

Madam Blavatsky taught me the *sissonne fondue* – a leap from both feet ending in something as close to unpowered flight as mankind can manage – and my *demi-plié* landing should be soft and pliant only it isn't because I slam into the back of the car and I'm hugging its smooth roundness and the car's gathering speed as it heads uphill, swaying wildly as the driver tries to dislodge me.

I feel myself slide as the car lurches. I hug in tighter as my fingers encounter ...

There's no air-conditioning so the back windows have to stay open, Vertical said. I work my hand around with little more to hold onto but hope, waiting for the lurch that will hurl me to my death.

There's a moment when all my weight's hanging on the little triangular window at the side of the car and my life's hanging by a thread as I find myself wondering how much filler gunk Vertical used to patch up the rust hole in the door and under my weight the door clicks onto its security latch as if debating whether to swing open completely and lose me or stay shut as the driver swings the steering wheel with the horn in the centre in an attempt to dislodge me. I'm too big to fit through the window, even if I could smack out the triangle of glass, but it doesn't matter because there's no headrest to the driver's seat, just as the car hasn't got seatbelts or airbags, and although my whitesides are dangling and the car's already up around the 50 mark – that's miles per hour not kilometres – I manage to get both hands around the driver's neck and hang on, which means he's going to die if he doesn't pull over because my fingers are around his trachea. The car's spinning to the left as the driver takes his hands off the wheel in an attempt to unloosen my grip at the same time as – by transverse reasoning – his right foot goes down on the accelerator and I see the brick wall rear up and there's nothing I can do but hang on and. The house behind the wall behind the fence reaches out for the Holden's nice chrome-plated grille and there's nothing I can do about that, either, nor about the car smashing through the brick wall into a bedroom full of pansy-coloured furniture, nor about the dame sitting up in bed, hands up over her mouth and her eyes wide open as …

The car's sideways on in the bedroom, hard up against the bed. I yell at the dame to get the hell out before the flames reach the petrol tank, drag out the driver and lay him on his back on a flowerbed. It's several days since he shaved and his head-hair's sprouting nicely.

He's staring up at me, his face drained both of blood and of revenge.

'You figured it out, didn't you?' he murmurs. 'I took you for an idiot which is why I gave you those files. But you're smarter than you look ...'

He gets all his words and phrases and tenses right as you'd expect an old-time journo to and he's still a tough-looking bugger but now he's a tough-looking bugger who's dying, his creased shirt collar awry and his face ashen while a portion of the big, chrome-plated FJ Holden steering wheel is sticking out of his chest and I tell him, *Yeah, I worked it out,* and his head falls back as his mouth and eyes fall open and he looks like he's talking to the moon.

'I thought I had it sorted ...' The words emerge in dribs and drabs, like the blood leaking from his chest: there are no Magiclips available and they wouldn't be much use even if there were, he's too far gone.

'It was a good disguise, pal – the best,' I tell him. 'You were no longer The Loved One – the little wife – but the nice, warm face of well-balanced journalism. And you were no longer someone who hated von Franck – you became his best friend and greatest admirer. What was clever was that in the intervening years you never tried to harm him, never showed how much you hated him, right up to the end. Instead, when you finally made your move, you killed other people in the belief that von Franck would be convicted of their murders. But Cock Robin's widow got blamed for his death.'

I keep talking, like it might somehow prolong life.

'When the investigation started to fade, an anonymous call from you alerted the cops to the significance of the shadow board and the possibility that von Franck was involved in Cock Robin's murder. The death of the cop ramped up the investigation but pointed it in the wrong direction. To make matters worse there was no evidence because I got rid of the wrench you planted at von Franck's. You set up that fight between von Franck and Clean Fill, with the idea of killing Clean Fill and framing von Franck for it. The photographer had to go because you were the one who told him about the fight and he was about to tell me ... Then, of course, it was Clean Fill's turn, complete with the coin on the carpet that you got Lofty and the Fat Lady to leave there to point to von Franck's involvement. And all the time you pretended to be von Franck's greatest admirer – which wasn't all that hard because you still loved him ...

'Meanwhile, I was busy removing your planted evidence and wrecking your attempts to frame von Franck – although at that stage I didn't realise who the murderer was, only that evidence was being planted. The Fat Lady and Lofty tried to frighten me off. When I came across them at von Franck's I thought they were von Franck's guards until I realised they weren't – because they were outside the house while the dog was inside. Then there was ...'

'Until I did what I should have done all along,' Curtis croaks, 'and gone for the jugular – *his* jugular – forgetting all about subtlety. Framing him didn't work because he was too lucky, too rich and too powerful, and also because you ...'

Like an ebb-tide, his face is fading from ash-grey to white; it won't be long; it had better not be long because the whole world's got mobile phones and soon all the neighbours will be taking photographs. Technology's the enemy of anonymity.

'The *girls*,' he man says. 'I'm sorry, my good friends, the Fat Lady and Lofty, did their best, but it wasn't enough, was it?' He frowns. 'Where are they now?'

'Dead,' I say.

'I thought they could be.' Every word's an agony but he still asks: 'How did they die?'

I tell him how they died and he winces.

'They did their best ... they were good friends who deserved a better fate than death.'

'Everyone dies.'

'Yes, but not by falling from the top of a ninety-storey skyscraper. I loved those two like the ex-lovers they were because we parted amicably. Unlike that other one' – he can't even say von Franck's name – 'The bastard who I loved with a passion, even after he dumped me, the man I called Tiny because he was big, while I was –'

I nod.

'Yeah, I know: *Blue.* I worked that out, too, Curtis.' I haul out the pretty-coloured picturegram he overlooked in the files and smooth it out, holding it up so that he can see von Franck and the dame with the red hair gazing into each other's eyes the way lovers do. 'He liked to be seen with women because in macho Australia it was good for business – he surrounded himself with nudie calendars and still made eyes at women but only for effect. Which is why he married Mrs Anonymous – because it looked good – and went on to fame and fortune while his ex-boyfriend – you – shaved off your lovely mop of red hair that resulted in your being called *Blue* and von Franck's naming his business after you – and you became bitter, twisted and vengeful.'

'Revenge is a dish best served cold,' Curtis murmurs.

Chapter 45

THE OTHER SIDE
OF THE COIN

I lower Curtis's head until it's resting on the rosebushes. He won't feel the thorns.

'What about the coin?'

'Ivan's only coin?' He manages a last smile and tries to reach in his pocket but fails. 'I can't,' he murmurs. 'Can you …'

I drag out a green bag. It's heavy – I assess its weight at maybe a kilogram – and when I upend it, hundreds of small, glittering coins spill out.

'He always said he only had one coin but he actually had hundreds. I got the Fat Lady and Lofty to seed Clean Fill's office with one of the many that Tiny gave me – in order to link von Franck with Clean Fill's coming murder. Except you took it, which meant there was nothing apart from the stoush and that wasn't enough …'

'Yeah,' I add as he pauses, 'a 1953 coin, recognisable because it was copper-coloured, while the 1952 coin – von Franck's one and only *real* coin, the one he habitually flipped – was more of a gold colour.'

'So you noticed that, too. He was too rich and powerful, wasn't he? And the police too slack, my luck too bad and you too smart for anything to stick. Leaving me with just the one option and that was to kill him myself and hang the consequences. I'd already bugged his phone to keep track of his movements – an old journo's habit – but you knew that, too, didn't you? You realised there was some other bugger ...' He allows himself another smile but it's weaker now. 'But how did you work out where we were?'

'The Fat Lady sang and after that I telephoned von Franck's wife for confirmation.'

Curtis sinks back for the last time. It's just as well because the sirens are almost upon us.

'What about Tiny? Is he –? Did I –?'

But it's Curtin's last byline.

I'm wearing the same coat I wore at the start of this caper as I swing by the lab. Through the mottled glass in the new-mended door I make out two figures. It's time to eat humble pie so I knock and after a while the boffin opens the door just far enough for me to see he's still big, still handsome and still smiling – although now there's something different about the smile.

'Ah, Detective,' he says. 'What a great time for you to call. I'm at a decisive stage in my latest experiment, having just made the discovery that logic, incorrectly applied, can be terribly misleading.' The red mark's still on his collar but I see now that it's ink. 'All my experimentation with rodents has gone to hell because rats don't buy flats ...'

We all make mistakes.

'Don't worry, Prof,' I say. 'Because I was wrong, too. Which is why I'm paying you a visit. You see, I deduced from all the available evidence that your assistant was to blame for the broken door and the mess, both in your lab and in your personal life, when all the time it wasn't her but a man named Curtis.'

I stop. The boffin's thrown open the door and the smile's still on his face and it's still a different smile but now I can see the mousy little woman – his wife – and she's smiling, too, at the same time as she's advancing towards me, her outstretched hand full of money.

'It's nice to see you,' she says, thrusting the dough at me. 'I wanted to thank you for what you did. If it hadn't been for you sowing the seed of doubt in Arthur's mind regarding that *Jezebel*, a *hands-off* relationship could have flowered into a *hands-on* one … As it is, not only are we closer than we've been in thirty years of marriage, but – after sacking Miss Anorexia – Arthur made me his assistant.'

Arthur's arm around his wife is protective and he's still smiling, only no longer at me. 'My lovely little Gorilla,' he murmurs.

I take it as my cue to depart.

I don't visit Annie – I've got to move on, unlike von Franck's boyfriend, John Curtis, who, before shaving off his red hair, was von Franck's lover and

– because of the hair – was known as *Blue*. I drop in on Aunt Rube to make sure she's still alive and after that pay a quick visit to Madam Blavatsky, the tinkle-tankle of Tchaikovsky greeting me – but no longer the *BLUEBIRD CONSTRUCTIONS* sign, which someone has replaced with a sign saying *FOR SALE*.

Upstairs I find Mismatch thumping away at the Steinway. Twenty or so grommets are scattered about the dance floor, going through the motions of dancing, while Madam B is shouting: *'One-two-one-two!'*

Mismatch is too engrossed in her task to look up, Madam B's got her back to me and the kids are too disciplined to tell her there's a man with blood all over him at the door, so I head back down the stairs.

He's sprawled at one of his customer-free tables, his legs outstretched and the bright sun of a new day lighting up his craggy features as he contemplates a fresh-minted copy of the *Daily Terrorgraph* while a mower rackets away in the background. Harry's Caff is a hole-in-the-wall with wall-to-wall disservice and coffee you drink only if you're tired of living. Harry believes in not doing any more than he has to and doing it often.

'So what's news, Mr High Energy?' I ask, sitting down.

He doesn't look up because that takes effort. Blood all over me? I could be a headless zombie for all

Harry knows. He shrugs his coathanger shoulders, keeping his eyes on the newspaper.

'Just another corpse in a graveyard,' he replies. 'Someone this rag refers to as vertical even though he was horizontal – if that makes any sense.'

'Nothing makes much sense in this world, Harry.' 'You of all people ought to know that.' The sound of the mower dies down. 'Was there just the one corpse?'

Harry shakes his head – or he could be trying to dislodge a fly.

'No, there were thousands. But in terms of fresh ones, no. Correction: there *was* one other body, with a steering wheel embedded in its chest, discovered not far from the cemetery – in an accident involving a bedroom, a dame and an FJ Holden. But it appears that the cops are treating it as an unrelated death while someone – there's a picture of him, a big man with his face deliberately pixilated and his name undisclosed because he can afford a good lawyer – is being held on suspicion of the murder of the man in the Holden.'

Harry looks up finally and notices the blood.

'Did you cut yourself shaving, Rainbow?'

I shake my head and at the same time, something – call it conscience or call it hope – makes me look towards the kerb where a dame is climbing off the pillion seat of a motor scooter cradling a babe while the rider's busy setting the bike back on its haunches. I turn my attention from the passenger to the pilot.

She's garbed entirely in black: flesh-cramping black tights, a black T-shirt that could be a first skin, a pair of high-polished black elastic-sided boots and a black full-face helmet, the visor turning multi-coloured as it swivels towards me, making my blood run colder than a lifetime of vengeance.

It's not just Harry's coffee that can kill you.

Also in the series

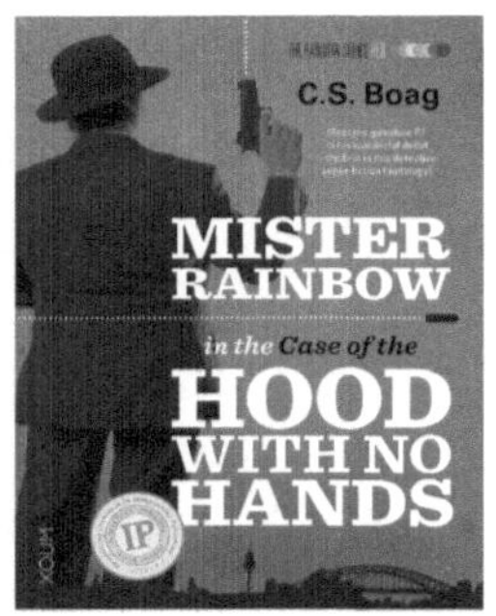

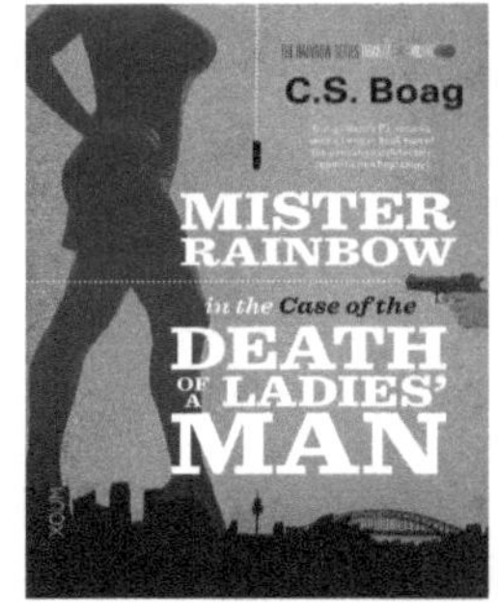

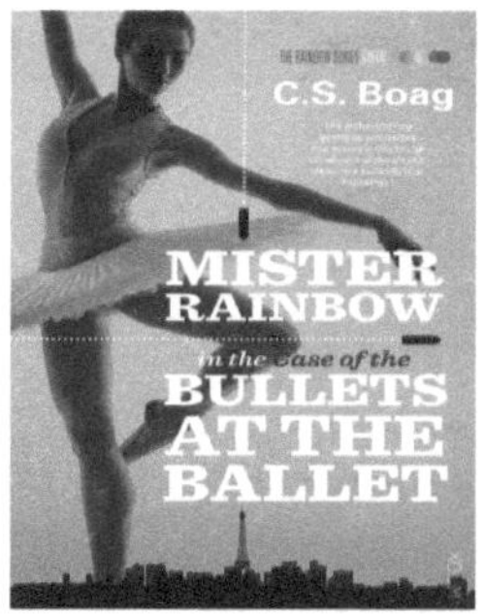

www.xoum.com.au